Stories about a Colorful Cast of Characters
Who Run and Patronize a Local Bagel Shop

Also by Eurice E. Rojas

Out of the Rough: The Cuban Revolution and Its Effect on Golf

Bagels & Cafecitos

...Life with a schmear

Eurice E. Rojas

LIFE TO PAPER
PUBLISHING

Copyright © 2024 by Eurice E. Rojas

All rights reserved. No part of this book may be reproduced by any mechanical, photographic, or electronic process, or in the form of a phonographic recording, nor may it be stored in a retrieval system, transmitted, or otherwise be copied for public or private use—other than for "fair use" as brief quotations embodied in articles and reviews—without the prior written permission of the publisher.

Caution: The central settings for the stories in this collection are the neighborhoods of Spanish Harlem and vicinity and on the New Jersey shore in times past and present. Character depiction and the use of "street" dialogue in some instances may be considered disrespectful or offensive. Readers are advised to approach the material with this in mind.

First Edition 2024

Paperback ISBN: 978-1-990700-67-5
eBook ISBN: 978-1-990700-66-8

Library of Congress Control Number: 2024917262

Cover design by Joe Potter
illustrations by Norma Almanza

Printed in the U.S.A.

1 2 3 4 5 6 7 8 9 10

Life to Paper Publishing Inc.
Toronto | Miami

www.lifetopaper.com

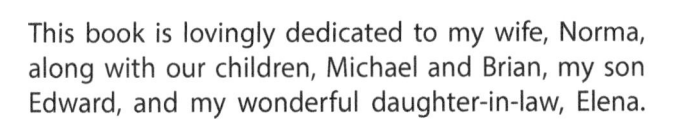

This book is lovingly dedicated to my wife, Norma, along with our children, Michael and Brian, my son Edward, and my wonderful daughter-in-law, Elena.

It is also in honor of my parents, Eurice and Onelia Rojas.

Contents

Dramatis Personae   x

Chapter 1   1

In which a life in the Old Country is exchanged for a life in the New, and the second generation commits to a venture that the reader will find endlessly entertaining.

Chapter 2   11

In which Esteban becomes a spy in a shop takeover bid and he, Maria, and Miguel embark on a journey to build new roots.

Chapter 3   20

In which Maria adds Cuban delicacies and cafecitos to an inspired menu and an unruly customer is treated to a lesson in common decency.

Chapter 4   31

In which Miguel comes to Mo's defense and averts a NYC showdown with roots as old as dust.

Chapter 5   39

In which Miguel faces a series of calamities, from a broken oven and forgotten suitcase to customers who don't want to pay their food bill.

Chapter 6   **48**

In which a Bruce Lee imitation is thwarted, and what sounds like the voice of God thunders in a certain neighborhood in Harlem late at night where Noel's dad's new Caddy attracts unwelcome attention.

Chapter 7   **67**

In which immersions into American culture include pilgrimages of some hundreds of miles and a few city blocks, tall tales, and the Rockettes.

Chapter 8   **81**

In which early weekend hours at the shop find Esteban entertaining ladies of the night and Vinny is saved by Maria, but with wiseguy consequences.

Chapter 9   **91**

In which a friend from the Dominican Republic shares stories from the streets of LA and to whom Miguel reveals the secret of how to "Americanize" a Spanish accent.

Chapter 10   **108**

In which a conman from North Jersey is treated like a hero when he's released for good behavior and tumbles Esteban to take over the shop to deceive none other than his own mother.

Chapter 11   **122**

In which Ditto finds a former friend from the neighborhood is muscling in on his business and Maria and Rosa come to Ditto's rescue.

Chapter 12   **134**

In which Esteban, Maria, and Miguel open the shop and their hearts when disaster strikes.

Chapter 13   **143**

In which Maria's attractive friend finds favor in an exclusive country club and Esteban resumes his spy skills at a Shiva to find a top-secret rugelach recipe.

Vignettes   **156**

In which the main characters insisted a few anecdotes be included.

Acknowledgments   **167**
About the Author   **169**

Dramatis Personae

Main Characters

The Fernandez family: Onaydis (mother) and Rolando (father), Cuban immigrants to the United States; Esteban, Maria, and Eduardo (siblings)

Miguel Alvarez: Cuban-American and Maria's husband

Marylin Fernandez: Esteban's wife

Gustavo "Ditto" Perez: Height-challenged Cuban gangster (à la Joe Pesci)

Noel Abramowitz: Jewish high school friend of Miguel

Papo: Dominican customer who has become Miguel's friend

Vinny Lombardi: Larger-than-life Italian restaurant owner and aspirational wiseguy

Bagel Shop Employees

Emil Sanchez: The bagel shop's promiscuous Mexican delivery man

Felipe: Salvadorian grill cook

Hector: Mexican grill cook who resembles a large brown bear

Jennifer: Irish deli server

Mohammed: Palestinian grill cook, called Mo for short

Pepe: Honduran bagel boiler and baker

Peter Garcia: Young Cuban-Chinese deli server

Incidental Characters

Bo: Head security guard at the Biltmore Hotel in Los Angeles

Harvey Muskowitz: The Rugelach King

Ismael: The thunderous voice of God and owner of a convenience store in Harlem

Jaime: Miguel and Maria's son

Julio Costa: Childhood friend of Ditto and fellow Cuban gangster

Magnus: Renowned street basketball savant and addict

Mickey: An obliging tow truck driver

Professor Rothenberg: Stoned high school chemistry teacher

Rosa: Ditto's cousin

Victor, Beatrice, and Ithañia: Friends of Maria and Miguel

Yolanda: Julio's estranged girlfriend and mother of his son

Chapter 1

In which a life in the Old Country is exchanged for a life in the New, and the second generation commits to a venture that the reader will find endlessly entertaining.

It was four p.m. on a hot Friday summer afternoon and staff at the bodega were as energetic as the syncopated Latino rhythms played by a transistor radio. It was a typical late-day frenzy with customers picking up foodstuffs they needed to prepare dinner. Hispanic families almost always prepared their meals from scratch as a sacramental exercise, and processed and frozen foods were shunned as neither culturally nor ideologically authentic. Canned food was limited to four-legged consumption.

"Onaydis, dame una libra de carne molida, por favor."

"Eso es todo, mi amor?"

"Sí, nada más. Gracias, Onaydis."

Although the customer had only asked for a pound of ground beef, Onaydis mentally checked off the orders from other regular customers she noticed who were patiently waiting in line. She knew that several were going to order quantities of steak to satisfy the appetites of male family members who boasted an ample waistline.

On the wall near the butcher counter was a black-and-white photograph of Onaydis and Rolando from 1958, portraying a happy young couple starting life together in their native Cuba. They lived on Onaydis's family farm, raising livestock and harvesting plantains from the groves. As life became difficult, they made the decision to leave Cuba with only what they could carry. They had talked about what a future in the United States might hold, and one of their dreams was to own a bodega, notwithstanding the fact that neither had any knowledge about running a retail food store. But their dream was strong, and their belief in an America where dreams could come true was even stronger. They reasoned that if they were able to overcome their exile from the imminent Cuban communist experiment, then nothing could stop them.

It was the early part of 1959 when they finally escaped to America and realized their dream of owning a bodega. The relentless determination, work ethic, and emotional connection to their community helped establish the bodega's reputation for fresh food at fair prices, and it became a popular gathering place. The store was located in such a highly dense Hispanic population pocket in New Jersey that it required a sign that stated "English is spoken here."

A circa-1963 rusted-steel desk fan furiously swirled behind the counter in a futile attempt to relieve the store of the soup of heat and humidity, and the fragrance of spices and aromas of foods. Above the soup rose the gossip being broadcast on Radio Bemba. (Radio Bemba is an expression that is applied to people that have a "big mouth," and is satirically recognized as a fictitious Spanish-language radio station that broadcasts gossip.) Carmen, a habitual customer, had brought the likelihood of another customer's infidelity to Onaydis's attention.

"No! What do you mean you don't think it's his baby?" questioned Onaydis.

"Sí, Onaydis. The baby doesn't look like him—the father!"

"What do you mean he doesn't look like his father? Does the baby look like his mother?"

"Un poquito," said Carmen, as she shrugged her shoulders.

Rolando was standing by the cash register, chuckling at the exchange between his wife and the resident Radio Bemba.

"Rolando! What are you laughing at?" squealed Onaydis.

"Es que, I've also heard rumors …"

Both women turned their focus on Rolando, hoping to hear more information.

"What have you heard, Rolando?" asked Carmen.

"Nada. Just that she buys a lot of chickens. What does the baby look like?"

Onaydis turned to the customer. "Have you seen the baby?"

"Sí, Onaydis."

"And?"

"He doesn't look at all like his father. You know her husband is Dominican and dark-skinned."

"Sí."

"The baby is very light-skinned."

"OK. Well, that doesn't mean anything. The mother is fair-skinned, so?"

"What is the shape of his eyes?" facetiously interjected Rolando, while displaying a shit-eating grin.

Carmen turned to Rolando, with a glimmer of understanding turning into a shocked expression. "Rolando, what do you know? Well … he has Chino eyes. There is not one drop of Dominican in that baby."

"How do you know this, Rolando?" probed an inquisitive Onaydis.

"Where do we buy our chicken, Onaydis?"

"In the store that slaughters live pollos down the street."

"Exacto. And I see the mother going to the chicken place a lot more than she needs to, and sometimes she buys chickens, and sometimes she goes home without any chickens."

"Sí, pero that doesn't mean anything, Rolando."

Rolando interrupted. "You go there and don't buy anything? Please … And who owns the chicken store, Onaydis?"

Carmen jumped in. "El Chino, Ito."

"Correcto. Ito the Chinese guy. But he is actually Japanese. And where does he live?" Rolando mockingly asked.

"Above the store," responded the customer, leading both women to demonstrably gasp while they simultaneously placed their right hand over their mouth.

"Ay, Dios mio, Rolando. Do you think …"

"Sin duda. Without a doubt."

"Rolando, I think you are right. He doessss look like Ito. He's 'baby Ito.'"

The customers who were eavesdropping laughed at the infidelity in their midst. Nearby was ten-year-old Maria, Onaydis and Rolando's daughter, restocking food items on denuded shelves. She had just returned from her ballet lesson and she nimbly pirouetted throughout the store, balancing cans of black and red beans. Customers could not fail to notice her boundless enthusiasm, sparkling dark eyes, and hair that framed an intelligent oval face.

It was just past four on a dreary late October evening in the bagel shop when Maria recalled the story of "Baby Ito" as a favorite memory of the bodega while contemplating where to hang the "heirloom" photograph of her parents. Dark, ominous clouds produced an incessant drizzle and an early darkness that obscured the street and discouraged customers from venturing out to the shop. Suddenly her husband, Miguel, came through the front door, shaking the damp off his suit.

Miguel had not told Maria he was coming by, in order to surprise her.

"Miguel, what are you doing here? You left work early?"

"I had a meeting scheduled at four today that I bailed from."

"Why did you not go to the meeting? Someone you don't like?"

"Besides my not liking this guy, whoever is dumb enough to set up a meeting at four p.m. on a Friday afternoon will never belong to a club I'd want to join. Besides, I thought you could use some help. We've only owned the shop for a whole forty-eight hours."

"Well, of course I'm glad you're here."

"I'm glad to trade this suit in for an apron and broom and mop, especially given that tomorrow is the first Saturday that we will face."

With no one in the store other than Maria, Miguel, and a couple of employees, the arrival of darkness and rain seemed to insulate the shop from the outside world. It made Miguel thoughtful. "Maria, remember where we were five years ago, pretty close to this date?" he asked.

"Not exactly. In the city? Where were we?"

"It was our anniversary, and we celebrated in Katz's Deli, and you straight up came out and said that one day you were going to own a deli like this."

Miguel noticed the photo of Maria's parents. "That's a really nice picture. Is that in Cuba?"

"It is Cuba, and that was their one-year wedding anniversary."

"We have much to thank them for, Maria. How old were you when they opened the bodega?"

"Six. You know, Miguel, when I was in eighth grade, I blew up at my brother because he was acting like a dictator, bossing me around to do stupid things in the bodega. He was such a jerk, and I swore that I would never work in the bodega ever again, especially with him. If you want proof of the irony of life, I'm a perfect example, because here I am now, part-owner of a bagel shop with two Cubans I'm related to through blood and marriage. And now my mother can't believe we're doing this. She still has PTSD from when they owned the bodega and how much work it entailed."

"Yeah, but the bodega paid for the private education you and your brothers enjoyed."

"Who could have predicted this, Miguel?"

"No shit. I never knew what a bagel was when I was young. It wasn't until I became a teenager and started hanging out with some Jewish friends that I had my first bagel—an onion bagel with cream cheese, to be exact."

"Damn, Miguel, you still remember that?"

"Like it was yesterday. I had never experienced a

bagel. I was a bagel virgin. And now it's in my highlight reel."

Maria responded, "Me either. We loved eating our Wonder bread, or Cuban bread, but never, ever did a bagel cross our paths."

Miguel laughed out loud and thoughtfully shared some of his favorite foods when he was young. "Maria, I would eat a bar of butter as if it were a Popsicle."

Maria squirmed at the thought as Miguel continued. "And I would eat hot dogs raw, as if they were bologna sticks. That stick of cured mystery meat was my version of beef jerky."

"My parents remind me of where we came from, and where we're capable of going next. This is a new chapter in life for us. For all of us." Tears welled up in Maria's eyes.

Concerned, Miguel took Maria's hand and stroked her hair. "What's the matter, honey?"

"Tomorrow is my parents' anniversary. And I wish my dad was still alive to see us doing this. I wish he would have been around to be with our kids."

She wiped away her tears.

Miguel delicately suggested, "How about hanging the photo above the coffee service? That will help tell our story. You are planting a flag declaring that we are, first and foremost, a family place."

"I like that. And we can leave colored markers there, and any customer that wishes to can write a comment on the wall."

"Beautiful, Maria."

It was now five o'clock, and the employees said their good nights. Maria and Miguel continued with the after-hours cleanup, which was just about completed when they heard a hard and insistent knock on the front door. Maria looked irritated and told Miguel to let the customer know they were closed for the day. Miguel was smiling as he unlocked the door to let Esteban in.

"Yo. We were just talking about you."

"What are you doing back here, Esteban? You've been at it since dawn," asked Maria.

"Just thought I would see what I could do to get a head start on tomorrow. The bakers start at three thirty tomorrow morning. What were you guys saying about me?"

Maria, with a flair for the dramatic, said, "That you were an asshole at the bodega, telling me and Eduardo what to do."

"Mom told me to be a boss, and I was an asshole, but here you are anyway."

"Sí, and here we are. Esteban, do you remember the story about the Chinese guy that owned the poultry slaughterhouse down the street from the bodega?"

"Well, yes, but he was Japanese, not Chinese, and he had a baby with the lady who was married to the Dominican guy. Right? Is that the way the story went?"

"Yes."

"Why do you bring this up, Maria?"

"I was just laughing to myself at all the crazy stuff that came to pass at the bodega. Do you know what happened to that kid? What was his name?"

"His name is Juan. He was given the Dominican father's name."

Maria burst into uncontrollable laughter, prompting a confused Miguel to ask, "Maria—what am I missing?"

"Well, his biological father, the guy who owns the slaughterhouse and had an affair with Juan's mother, was named Ito."

"And …"

"So, his name is Juan, but it's very common for people named Juan to have a nickname."

Esteban gleefully interjected, "Everyone, intentionally or otherwise, called him by his new name—Juan-ito. Juanito. Maybe there is some truth in gossip after all."

"And now he's running the slaughterhouse, right, Esteban?"

"Irony of ironies, he inherited the slaughterhouse and, yes, he is running it. He has a nice Porsche 911 too. Custom color off-white. Like all his chickens."

The storytelling was interrupted by a flurry of knocks at the front door. Esteban opened the door to welcome a delivery of pizzas and other Italian delicacies. Maria stood up with a puzzled look on her face when friends, old and young, poured into the shop.

"What the hell are all of you doing here?" she exclaimed.

"Mama, we're here to bless your store and have dinner. You know, like when people christen a boat before they launch it, or escape from Cuba. Didn't Esteban or Miguel tell you?" said one of Maria's closest friends, Isabella, as she smothered Maria with a damp and escape-proof bear hug.

Maria was able to momentarily squirm out of Isabella's affectionate headlock and, with mock disbelief, said to Miguel and Esteban, "You two knew about this?"

Their grins affirmed their guilt as coconspirators, and they turned to welcome their guests.

Maria noticed her friend was carrying an ornate little bottle with a clear liquid in it. "Isabella, what do you have with you? What is that? Don't tell me …"

"Mija, tengo agua bendita para bendecir la tienda."

"You're going to bless the store with holy water?" Maria was touched by her sentiment.

"Of course, Maria. To protect you guys and the store."

Maria lifted her right hand over her heart, saying, "Gracias, Isabella. I love you. Thank you." She looked at Miguel. "Tomorrow is our first Saturday, and it will be very interesting to see how everything goes. Do you think we can make a go of this? Truly?"

"Mi amor, if you've made it this far, we are not going to fail. Think about it. Our families escaped from Cuba, and you and your brothers worked in the bodega with your parents. My folks were able to work their way out of Spanish Harlem. We didn't come this far to fail, baby. Have no doubt."

The evening wore happily on and the clouds departed, leaving a clear sky. With the holy water benediction done, Maria affectionately took hold of Miguel's and Esteban's arms and softly said, "Let's go home, guys. Fresh start tomorrow. Who knows what the day will bring?"

"And the day after that," chimed in Miguel.

"And the day after that," echoed Esteban.

CHAPTER 2

In which Esteban becomes a spy in a shop takeover bid and he, Maria, and Miguel embark on a journey to build new roots.

A few months earlier, Emil had spilled the beans to Esteban that the bagel shop was being put up for sale. Emil was one of the delivery guys for the store, and he happened to engage in a casual conversation with a customer by the name of Esteban while stocking one of the fridge displays.

"Do you have any sugar-free Snapple?" asked Esteban, as he scoured the fridge display for his preferred beverage. It was a hot and humid June afternoon, and Esteban had dropped by the shop on his way home.

"No. The Snapple guy hasn't been around for a week," returned Emil, which prompted a cynical response from Esteban.

"Ha, ha, ha. Why not? You guys haven't paid your bills?"

Emil rose from his squat, wiped his right hand on his apron, and introduced himself. "My name is Emil."

Although taken by surprise, Esteban cordially responded, "Nice to meet you, Emil. Me llamo Esteban. Coñjo, Emil. You don't have many juices either! What is going on in this place, dude?"

"Dis place is not in bueno shape. Dey always late to pay vendors and dey treat us like shit."

"That does not sound bueno, Emil."

"No, but I hope dings will be better because de owners are dinking of selling dis place, and maybe better owners will buy it."

"Wait … this place is going up for sale?" Emil had sparked Esteban's curiosity.

"They're talking about it for real, Señor Esteban, so I think so."

"Does anyone know about this? Have they advertised it, Emil?"

"No, no, no. Not yet."

"How's the business here, Emil? It doesn't look busy."

"No, business is no bueno because de owners are muy malo. Dey treat customers bad and employees bad."

After conducting an informal investigation with Emil for several more minutes, Esteban left the bagel shop without a drink, but he had gained some meaningful intelligence and, he hoped, an unexpected friend and ally. He couldn't wait to tell Maria and Miguel about what he had accidentally learned about the bagel shop.

"What do you mean they're selling the bagel shop? How'd you find out?" asked Maria.

"Are you talkin' about the shop next to the Hudson River?" added Miguel. "The one just south of the George Washington Bridge?"

"Yes, Miguel. That one. The shop in the strip mall by the river."

"Holy shit."

"I stopped in to get a Snapple and the delivery guy was there fillin' up the fridge. His name is Emil. He said the place is not doing well. That it sucks to work there and the owners treat the staff and customers like shit."

Miguel smirked at Esteban. "Then why would we want to buy this?"

"Because we can turn it around," enthused Maria. "We can turn that place into a destination breakfast and lunch place. Just like a real New York deli nosh."

"True. There are a lot of New York people who have relocated around these communities," offered Miguel.

"I hate to point out the obvious, but it's a Jewish deli. What the hell do we know about running a Jewish deli? It's not a Cuban restaurant or a bodega," said Esteban.

"Maybe we could also sell Cuban food," suggested Maria.

The three sat quietly for a time, staring at one another as they contemplated the door opening to a life-altering event that felt like their destiny. Esteban broke the silence. "We need more information—a lot more. Plus, we don't even know yet if they're actually selling the place, so let's not get ahead of ourselves."

"Are you going to ask the owners if they're going to sell?" prodded Maria.

"Not right away. What I'm going to do is give Emil a hundred bucks and keep talking to him, and start hanging around the store more to get a sense of customer traffic."

"You're basically conducting a stakeout like an undercover cop," said Miguel.

"Or a stalker," said Maria, laughing.

"Stakeout or stalker, we'll contact the owners once all the info has been assembled and we all agree on what to do next," said Esteban.

• • •

Esteban led the intelligence gathering by visiting the store at different hours of each day, every day, for the better part of a month, and observing the ebb and flow of customer traffic along with employee interactions. He subsequently returned to Maria and Miguel to offer his observations and recommendations. They soon shared his enthusiasm for becoming the owners of a bagel shop.

Esteban was able to confirm that the store was bleeding money. He crafted his approach to the owners and made a soft pitch, not expecting much in the way of a firm response. But that's not what happened. The owners even named a price—non-negotiable—and agreed to allow Esteban to begin his due diligence.

Esteban was soon reviewing end-of-day receipts, taking inventory, and speaking with key suppliers as part of his due diligence. Over the course of another month or so, he saw how the owners (who, ironically, were not Jewish) ran the store like a sweatshop, with little respect or regard for their employees. The owners even kept all the service tips for themselves. "We own the place, so it's our money—not yours" was a dictum Esteban heard more than a few times from the store's matriarch. Maria, Esteban, and Miguel prepared for a hostile response when it came time to open up negotiations.

On an almost daily basis, Esteban, Maria, and Miguel convened to discuss Esteban's intelligence, including what was being mismanaged and fixable, and how their negotiation strategy might play out. First, they made a list of the pros and cons:

Pros:
1. A promising location, though that was a factor the owners could use to jack up the sale price. The store was ideally located in a fashionable, burgeoning community filled with many young high-income professionals who were, until recently, NYC apartment dwellers. Apart from their innate affinity for really good city bagels, these customers were a big pick-up-and-delivery base that preferred not be inconvenienced by having to use their kitchen other than to open the refrigerator to take out leftover delivery food.
2. The store's reputation for mediocre to bad food and rude service, a factor in their favor, to negotiate the price down.
3. They could expand the menu with Cuban food.
4. Opportunity, opportunity, opportunity.
5. Their unstoppable attitude.

Cons:
1. Considerable work to reconstruct trust with employees and customers.
2. Operational fixes—how expensive and time consuming?
3. Local customers who see the store as nothing more than an architectural blight and a last-resort convenience.
4. A need to resolve service issues and introduce a new customer culture.
5. Accounts payable issues with suppliers to address.
6. Possible hard-line negotiation.

The day came when after ping-ponging the pros and cons amongst themselves, Maria forced the issue. "Are we doing this, or not?"

"Not for the price they want," said Esteban. "The price has gotta align with revenue, and they have overstated their revenue because their end-of-day receipts don't add up to what they're asking for."

"How much cash are we putting on the table, Esteban?" Miguel asked.

"Twenty percent of the purchase price. The usual shit, Miguel."

Miguel continued, "What's the difference between what they want for the shop and what the receipts tell us?"

"About eighty thousand a year. About sixty-five hundred a month that they're short, Miguel. So, if we paid what they want, we'd be losing eighty thousand right off the bat."

"Do we have the money to put down fifty percent instead of just twenty?" asked Maria.

"Yes, we could. We can lay down fifty percent cash," confirmed Esteban. Then he said, "I see where you're going."

"Tell them to bring the purchase price down to match the receipts. There is no customer goodwill, so that's off the table. Discount the eighty thousand and we'll lay down fifty percent cash on the deal," suggested Miguel.

Maria nodded approvingly.

Esteban confirmed what they were all thinking. "Then let's try it. Agreed?"

At the next meeting, Esteban presented their offer. After the initial shock and awe—which the trio knew going in was all pretense—the deal was accepted pending one final condition. Some of the inventory was found to have been spoiled, and the shyster owners had to grudgingly hand over a refund to the Cubans. Deal done.

And so it was that Maria, Esteban, and Miguel embarked upon a monumental spiritual, psychological, and cultural culinary metamorphosis. Who cared if they were Cuban and didn't have any experience operating a bagel shop and deli serving Jewish items? They were convinced their energy and determination would overcome any shortcomings from their lack of expertise and knowledge. Of course, an integral part of this exercise would entail earning the trust and respect of the employees and building a sense of family.

As Esteban had observed, the crew at the store was an eclectic melting pot of misfits, and they were united by a need to get along with one another and their deeply felt disdain for the owners. The origins of the steady employees spanned the globe: three grill cooks were from Palestine, Italy, and Mexico; six deli servers were from El Salvador, Mexico, Ireland, Cuba, and Puerto Rico (not recruited from or associated with H&H Bagels); the roller was a Spanish guy; and the bagel cook was Honduran. The rest of the employees were per-diem workers who also hailed from one of the above-mentioned countries, not to mention that the three new owners were Cuban-American.

The bagel shop and its team story seemed destined to be a food-service rendition of the movie *The Bad News Bears*. It was a venture that was going to require exceptional patience and diplomacy on the level of the United Nations to relate to their employees and try to meet their needs and the goals they aspired to, along with managing a diverse customer population. Most importantly, the new owners would have to reframe the "let's just get along so we can get through another day at work" way things were done and inspire trust and hope amongst the workers.

They were convinced that the way to transform the store into a gastronomical utopia for customers was through the hearts of their employees.

At the end of the day, the three of them felt the store was underperforming on multiple fronts and were confident they could pull it out of the abyss it found itself in. They all brought unique talents to the work ahead. Although Maria and Esteban were currently managing other businesses, they had the flexibility to bring their energy and resources to rejuvenating the shop.

Maria represented the cumulative creative spirit of the three. She was a graphic designer, a painter, and, most importantly, a religious foodie who possessed a meticulous level of precision for the quality of the food the shop would offer. She also had other talents related to the culinary industry, as she had professionally managed a couple of noteworthy chefs with promotional and public relations projects. Maria would be responsible for enhancing the shop's culinary appeal, physical appearance, and overall customer experience.

Esteban had been a controller for a prominent hedge fund on Wall Street and fit the stereotypical profile of an accounting assassin. Relentlessly detail-oriented, with eyes that would penetrate someone's soul and unveil their bullshit, he was slated to fill the role of the financial commander. Armed with a pocket protector as his gladiator's shield, Esteban would be akin to an IRS Special Forces agent, overseeing purchasing, operations, and accounting.

Miguel would only be able to contribute on weekends, performing as a master of ceremonies by taking orders and engaging with customers. In sum, the three would collectively take the stage as hosts of the shop, especially on weekends, when the store was a beehive of customer activity. Their drive to be successful was an inherited connection among the three: the resilient DNA possessed by their courageous parents, who had escaped their native country with only their clothes on their back to foster new roots in America.

Four months after Emil had told Esteban about the shop, it was now theirs. The romance was over and the magical mystery ride was about to begin. It was a Pepto-Bismol, Tums, and Alka-Seltzer moment—the trifecta of the stomach Olympics, as their intestines started to churn from the anxiety of the unknown. Wordlessly (a state of shock does that to you), they each started to clean a different part of the store. After a time, Maria paused her sweeping, straightened up, and exclaimed, "What the fuck have we gotten ourselves into?"

Then she twirled and lifted her broom above her head, dancing to a Cuban syncopation in her head. Miguel and Esteban joined in.

CHAPTER 3

In which Maria adds Cuban delicacies and cafecitos to an inspired menu and an unruly customer is treated to a lesson in common decency.

"I want to add some Cuban foods to the menu. Everyone loves Cuban food."

The kitchen had been under Maria's command for a few short months, and she always had a passion for sharing her Cuban roots and her love of Cuban food with customers. She was convinced that the store needed to shake up the menu, for a couple of reasons. Making sure she had Esteban's attention, she said, "Look. We can offer some Cuban café staples like some desserts, empanadas, and sandwiches. You know—some typical Cuban café stuff."

"Don't forget Cuban coffee," said Esteban.

Maria, Esteban, and Miguel were foodies and united in their conviction that the quality of the food they prepared for their customers had to be at the same level as or exceed what they expected from any of their favorite restaurants. Maria insisted that most everything be made fresh in-house. And if it wasn't made in-house, then items had to come from premium suppliers.

Maria continued, "We have to expand the client base with more diverse items, including adding to the Jewish deli repertoire, and we can also start branding the store with merchandising items and loyalty rewards. Don't forget that we have a big network of friends and business associates, and we need to tap into those relationships. And we need to get locals wanting to come here also."

"The prices will go up slightly," Esteban said, "but it'll be worth it because the customers aren't going to be able to find this quality anywhere else. They would have to go into the city, and we want to avoid that by offering customers what they would normally find across the river right here in their backyard."

Maria saw food as an art form much like dance and painting. Her professional curiosity about cuisine had been activated when she worked as a talent agent representing several chefs that were ambitiously seeking popular acclaim in the celebrity chef arena. Despite having little experience in the food business, she used her unrelenting chutzpah to secure invites for these chefs to be featured at the legendary James Beard House, and also managed to infiltrate the Food Network to arrange auditions for new shows that were being produced. That professional exposure encouraged a passion she had only imagined in her life—an opportunity to apply her creative, artistic talents to cuisine.

Maria loved making people happy, and felt that food and happiness were sisters. Good food enjoyed around a table was akin to a spiritual experience, firing the senses. Food brought people together and reminded everyone of shared values and family history. This came by way of telling stories, because when Maria and her family emigrated from Cuba, family and friends gathered at dinnertime to share their experiences, and hopes and dreams. And now the bagel shop had become her canvas, and she had at her disposal all the resources she would need to create her culinary gallery of exquisite flavors to make even the most discriminating taste bud cry out for more.

The trio agreed to revise the menu and proceeded to delete marginally requested items, weave in Cuban favorites, create new items, and expand the range of Jewish delicacies. Their goal was to appeal to a larger customer base, and the new menu would also serve as a declaration to the public that the shop was unmistakably under new management. The most culturally conspicuous new item on the menu would be the inclusion of Cuban coffee, and in time it would become the most wildly popular item in the new lineup, so much so that on weekends Maria had to train employees as baristas so they could appropriately concoct the complex Cuban cafecitos.

And customers couldn't get enough of the buzz, literally and figuratively, as they illogically reasoned that as long as their bagels were scooped all the way down to the outer crust, they could lavishly foray into the exotic range of hot and cold Cuban coffee experiences—and not feel they were cheating on their diets. Cuban stalwarts rejoiced at the traditional applications of Cuban coffee, while others new to the enlightenment were taken hostage by their discovery of a new type of caffeine that, happily, seemed to carry an extra jolt of enthusiasm.

Other efforts to increase the business included actively participating in public relations and community grassroots promotional activities. In the proceeding months, Esteban, Miguel, and Maria had been featured favorably in news articles, and in addition, they built relationships with schools and faith-based organizations from their community and beyond. They also started merchandising the shop with customized t-shirts and canvas bagel bags.

The new additions to the menu created opportunities to upsell ordinary purchases. For example, many new items were placed near multiple checkout stations, enabling the cashier to cajole the customer into adding to their original order. This turned out to be a hugely successful revenue-generating tactic, as customers, more often than not, couldn't resist purchasing additional freshly baked goods at their point of sale. Maria and Esteban trained the cashiers to politely and personably highlight the tasty benefits of complementing their original order with side items. The cashiers would say, "You know what would go great with that Italian hero? This beautiful rice pudding that was just made!" Or "These guava empanadas just came out of the oven and would be perfect to follow up your bacon, egg, and cheese." And "The banana pound cake is still warm. Get a piece for now, or later."

Engaging customers in a casual, friendly conversation as they were checking out also created opportunities to build relationships of trust and camaraderie. It was as if the employees had become personal shoppers for the customers. The tactic significantly increased sales, because most customers would happily spend an additional five or ten dollars more than their original order.

Six months had passed and customers and employees alike were still acclimating to the new management policies and store makeover, and while many welcomed the improved quality of food and attention to cleanliness and courteous customer service, there were customers who were not so easily impressed. Esteban had predicted that a new culinary experience would come at a cost. For some doleful customers, a ten percent increase across the board was too heavy a cross to bear. In strict business terms, the retail prices had been increased to cover the increased costs associated with purchasing foodstuffs from vendors who offered higher-quality provisions. Esteban, who took the lead in dealing with the food suppliers, had opened discussions with new purveyors who provided premium-grade foods. Consequently, only one-quarter of the previous suppliers continued to do business with the bagel shop.

Some customers even squabbled about the ten-dollar minimum before a credit card could be used for their purchase. "Any purchase under ten dollars has to be cash," explained Esteban as a customer was taking out his credit card to pay for a four-dollar bagel sandwich.

"Whaddya mean? I gotta buy ten dollars' worth of shit to use my card?"

"Yup. That's what the sign says. Ten dollars."

"That's bullshit, and it's illegal."

"You mean to tell me that you don't have four bucks in your pocket?"

"No, as a matter of fact, I don't. Is there a law that says I have to have four bucks in my pocket?"

"No, there is no law that you're required to carry four bucks in your wallet. Unless you're talking about a common-sense law that you should always have some cash in your pocket. But what law are you referring to that makes what I'm doing illegal? Are you a lawyer? Because if you are, you're not a good one, because, first of all, you don't know the law, and second, you don't even have enough cash for a four-dollar bagel." With one leg up on a stool like the swashbuckler on a Captain Morgan rum label, Esteban had used the fingers on his right hand for emphasis to denote the numbers one and two as he made his point. He had also anticipated situations like this, which had prompted him to install an ATM and joyfully take in a commission on every transaction.

"C'mon. You gotta be kidding me! What the fuck, dude? I don't have four bucks. Can't you cut me some slack?"

The customer hadn't bothered to say please, but it wouldn't have mattered, as Esteban directed his gaze to, and motioned toward, the new ATM.

Now I'm going to make more money off you for being stupid and obnoxious, thought Esteban. Esteban was an old-school guy who was taught early on a pragmatic and valuable lesson by his parents: Never leave the house without having at least fifty bucks in your pocket or stuffed in your socks. The logic behind this was simple: If he ever got into some kind of trouble, cash was universal and could meet any situation.

Esteban was an acolyte of the "money talks and bullshit walks" school of fiscal wisdom. He even had the expression monogrammed on his pillow cases. In Esteban's mind, money would always talk—no bullshit.

Esteban dryly stated, "There's an ATM over there if you want to get cash."

The customer unconsciously reacted to Esteban's finger-pointing, turning his head toward the ATM, only to respond, "C'mon, man! That fucker is going to charge me ten percent on my twenty bucks. C'mon, cut me a break and let me use the card, please."

Esteban took note of the customer using the word *please*. The capitulating request for help garnered favor with Esteban, and as he quickly thought through the request, he decided on a strategic and empathetic solution.

"This is what we're going to do."

The customer anxiously awaited Esteban's decision.

"You can't use a credit card to pay for your bagel."

The customer bristled and moved to respond, but Esteban interjected. "Stop. Wait. Let me finish. You can take the sandwich and not pay for it today. When you have the cash, four dollars cash, come back and you can pay then."

The customer, while taken aback by the generous gesture, promised Esteban he would return the following day with the cash. "I really appreciate this, man. Thank you."

"And don't be a wise guy and come back to pay with coins!"

The gamble paid off in a unique way, as the next day, the customer reappeared during lunch hour but still did not have the cash to pay for the sandwich. Rather, he ordered lunch for himself and some co-workers, amounting to thirty dollars' worth of food. He then asked Esteban to also include yesterday's four-dollar charge on his credit card.

Esteban couldn't help but laugh at the irony of the situation and the customer's way of resolving the matter of high finance.

"Will you take my card now?" asked the customer.

"Glad to ring you up, my man. Appreciate your gesture."

"Thank you for trusting me," replied the customer.

"Of course. There was no reason not to trust you unless you gave me a reason not to trust you. But here you are! ... Oh shit, dude. I hate to tell you this, but your card has been declined. Wait. Let me try it again."

The customer's eyes began twitching, and his

mouth gaped as if he were having a stroke. "What? No way. That card can't be declined."

The card had actually been accepted, but Esteban could not resist having a little fun at the customer's expense.

"Nope. Got rejected for a second time. Do you have another card? Or, God forbid, any cash?"

The customer looked very flushed. Not wanting to have to call EMS, Esteban said, "Just kidding, buddy. The card went through the first time. Just fucking with you. We're good."

The customer began breathing again, smiled, and went back to his colleagues.

At the other side of the store, an employee named Peter, who had Chinese features, was verbally wrestling with a young woman, presumably also Chinese, who was upset that her sandwich had taken too long to make. She claimed the store had contempt for Asians. "I know they're racist here because they ignored me, and other people that ordered after me got their stuff before I did."

Peter apologized and assured her that no one was racist. It was simply that the grill had been backed up because the store was very busy. The customer could clearly see he had her sandwich in hand, but he pointed out the obvious anyway as he deposited the sandwich in front of her. "I have your order here, ma'am."

Apparently inconsolable, the woman appealed to the shop's clientele and continued to loudly voice her allegations. "I mean, whoever made this," she said, picking up the sandwich and waving it back and forth as if she were directing traffic, "has a problem with Chinese people. I mean, *you* must know how I feel. You know what I mean, right?"

Peter was a young man who was working at the

store to earn money to pay for his master's degree. He had been hired by Esteban, whom he had known since infancy because his dad and Esteban were close friends. Peter happened to be working on the grill making sandwiches that day and had prepared the young lady's order. He was also a descendant of a Cuban cultural phenomenon—a genetic mix of Cuban and Chinese ancestry.

Cuba at one time boasted the largest Chinese population in the Caribbean. The first wave of the Chinese exodus to Cuba was tied to the island's sugar plantations and the need for workers. Unfortunately, the laborers were regarded as indentured servants. They worked in unrelenting heat and humidity, and after their typical eight-year contract was up, most could not pay for the return trip to China. Even some who could afford to leave chose to stay on the island.

The second wave of Chinese immigrants to Cuba came from California, many of them merchants hoping to establish small businesses. More arrived when Cuba softened its immigration laws after the First World War, and when the Chinese Communist Party formally established the People's Republic of China in 1949, prompting many Chinese to flee the country and travel to Cuba, where they had family ties.

Having successfully assimilated into a new country far removed from their origins, the Chinese population embraced Cuban culture and comingled their traditional values with a Cuban lifestyle, including cuisines and speaking Spanish. Even today, it is not unusual to go to a Cuban-Chinese restaurant featuring a menu of Cuban and Chinese fusion plates and operated by generational Chinese owners who speak fluent Spanish.

Another lady, one table over, interrupted the

conversation to ask Peter in Spanish for a plastic knife and fork.

"Disculpame. Me puede dar un tenedor y cujillo, por favor?"

"Seguro, señora. Aquí tienes."

As Peter handed the utensils over, the Chinese lady appeared confused and asked, "Wait, you speak Spanish? Aren't you Chinese?"

"My family background is Chinese. My parents are Cuban-Chinese. And I'm a Cuban-Chinese American."

"But you have a Chinese accent."

"I know. I watch a lot of Jackie Chan movies."

"Do you speak Mandarin or Putonghua?"

"No, but I can read fortune cookies when pushed, and I can sing 'Guantanamera' in Spanish. And, through on-the-job training, I am also currently learning the lyrics to 'Hava Nagila' in Hebrew."

The Chinese lady sensed she was being mocked and began to admonish Peter for working in an establishment that was bigoted toward Chinese people. "I bet they treat you like a second-class citizen, because if they treat me like this, then I can't imagine what you have to put up with."

"Lady, stop. No one is a racist here. I don't know where you are coming up with this stuff. Everyone here is a minority. And they're all working hard, trying to make a living. Also, the owners of this joint treat me and all of us like family. It doesn't matter that I am Cuban-Chinese American, or that Pedro's Mexican, or that Gabriele is from Guatemala, or that Denny is the shop's potato-peeling Irishman. If anyone is berated about being a second-class Lucky Charms, it's that leprechaun over there."

"I can hear what you're saying, Babalu!" said Denny, laughing, as he stacked bags of flour. This kind of banter between the staff occurred frequently in an attempt to humanize—and satirize—all the stereotypes and racism they had encountered throughout their lives. Denny continued his volley at Peter. "Did you take an Uber rickshaw to work today, Pedro?"

The customer quickly escalated from feeling slighted to aggravated beyond reason. *Road rage* became *racism rage*. "I won't take any more of this. I want to speak with the manager!"

Esteban had been watching the incident unfold and quickly edged up to her table. "I happen to be the acting manager. And Peter happens to be a valued employee, and he prepared your sandwich to order. So, as you can plainly see, racism against Chinese people, or anyone, does not happen in my store."

"Then I don't understand. What took you so long to prepare my sandwich? I mean, it's not like it's a hard sandwich to put together."

Peter smiled. "You're right. It's not a complicated sandwich."

"Then what took so long?"

"I put it together using chopsticks."

CHAPTER 4

In which Miguel comes to Mo's defense and averts a NYC showdown with roots as old as dust.

Our trio of new shop owners knew what was in store for them: the shop was unsanitary; inventory levels had not been managed properly and so large amounts of food products were shamelessly going to waste; the staff weren't exactly customer-friendly; and one of the three proprietors had to be certified by the municipality to provide food items to the public.

To add to their to-do list, Esteban began noticing that customers were getting different-sized portions for their orders, totally at the staff's discretion. Favored customers would receive close to a pound of deli cuts in their sandwiches, while the less-favored would get half that amount—and for the same price. In essence, staff were liberally "free pouring"—akin to what bartenders do—deli meats.

Esteban and Maria soon put a stop to the favored status of the few. As they expected, the customers who had become accustomed to the largesse wasted no time in expressing their displeasure through verbal abuse, which Esteban and Maria also kiboshed.

The shop soon had standardized measurements for all food items as ingredients and final product sale. Not only that, the bagel shop team was convened and given a new bilingual playbook, which outlined the new policies that would hopefully help turn the shop into a profitable one. It was a new day, and the shop would be known by its high quality of food and service, and as a place where the employees were proud to work. Miguel also added, "And you will share the tips amongst yourselves at the end of each day. Tips are yours. Not ours."

Only a couple of employees nodded their head affirmatively, and the rest seemed confused. The ambivalent reactions from the employees were not altogether encouraging. Miguel interpreted their reaction to be a guarded wait-and-see, actions-speak-louder-than-words attitude.

"What about police officers and what they order?" asked Jennifer, an older employee who lived in the community and was on a first-name basis with most of her customers.

"Police officers get treated like anyone else. Ten percent discount. That's it."

"Ooohhhh," said Jennifer. "They're not going to like that. Cops are gonna stop coming here."

Esteban was clear. "We're not in the business to lose money, Jennifer. If they stop coming, we'll come out ahead. Hopefully, they will appreciate the upgrade in the quality of the food. But if not, we're still better off."

Jennifer shook her head disapprovingly. She wasn't alone.

"They gonna tell other people not to come. Like all the people that work for the town. The fire department and the guys that do the garbage," said Felipe, one of the grill cooks.

"I understand," responded Esteban. "But we can't depend on just those people to make this work. All the discounts leave us with little to no money, and it also means that they are taking up time and resources that should be directed at customers who don't receive discounts or extra food. We can't discount our way out of this, and we have to attract customers that have otherwise not come to this shop because of its terrible reputation." He let his words sink in, then continued, "You are all part of the new direction. One of us will always be here to support you at the shop, every day. We hope you'll all get on board and help turn this place around."

The conviction displayed by Esteban seemed to hypnotize the employees, as if he were a preacher conducting a religious performance for his congregation. He was hoping for an *amen* at the end of his inspirational monologue, but instead got a question from Mo. "Mo" was short for Mohammed. He topped out at five-foot-three—a demure guy but one who, as the trio was to discover, worked his ass off, every day.

"We keep the tips?" His inflection betrayed his suspicion.

"Every cent. Does anyone else have any questions?"

Pepe, who baked the bagels, spoke up. "Tu va estar aquí a las tres y media de la mañana cuando abramos?"

"Sí, Pepe. We will be here todos los días at three thirty in the morning with you, yes."

"Todos los días?" repeated Pepe.

"Every day means every day," reaffirmed a courteous, but stern, Esteban.

Esteban wrapped up the meeting. "Gracias a todos."

• • •

Esteban, Maria, and Miguel had bought the shop knowing that one of them had to acquire a food service license and certification, which involved taking courses and passing an exam. In addition to the precious time they had spent to get the shop up to speed, to satisfy customers it was *under new management*, the license was a crucial piece of the puzzle. Maria volunteered to go through the training. Esteban and Miguel responded with a collective sigh of "Thank you, God" in harmonic unison.

While Maria pursued her certification, Esteban was able to hire a grill cook from another shop who had the requisite health certification. And although this allowed them to have a certified person on site, two certifications were needed so that the shop could operate seven days a week, every day of the year.

After getting the employees onside, revising quality, sanitary, and customer service standards, and building new relationships with all the suppliers and vendors, the Cuban clan was now prepared to sell lox, an assortment of cream cheeses, tuna fish, egg and chicken salads, sturgeon, soups, a hell of a lot of breakfast and hot-and-cold deli sandwiches, and even Cuban food, to an unsuspecting audience. *What planet am I on?* thought Esteban. *We're a Cuban family that has accepted the challenge of running a bagel shop and Jewish-type deli, and supplying hand-rolled bagels to a lot of neighboring bagel shops. It doesn't make any sense.*

A run-in with a customer was inevitable with the introduction of new food items, but no one could have predicted the sizable escalation of one particular incident. It happened on a Saturday. A big, burly guy, who could have held his own in any WWE-sanctioned cage match, had just gotten his sandwiches and within seconds demanded to see the manager, which happened to be Miguel. As Miguel approached him, he easily measured the customer's level of aggravation by his contorted facial expression, accompanied by copious beads of sweat streaming down his forehead, as if he were being held hostage by a stubborn episode of constipation. Facing the customer, separated by a glass counter, was Mo.

Miguel tucked Mo behind him and tried to put some distance between himself and the sweat and spittle spraying from the dude's mouth. "This fucking idiot"—he pointed at Mo—"put a hot sandwich and a bagel with *cold* cream cheese in the same bag." Miguel tried to process the mastodon's dilemma. At first, Miguel did not understand what the problem was—until common sense prevailed: "Why would a hot sandwich be placed in the same bag as cold cream cheese? I get it now." He turned to Mo to ask him what was going on. Mo admitted it was a stupid thing to do, apologized to the customer and Miguel, and with another bag in hand, offered to place one of the sandwiches in a separate bag or make a new bagel-and-cream-cheese sandwich.

Mo was squirming and visibly shaken by the possibility of a hostile and potentially life-ending physical assault. As Mo spoke with Miguel, his eyes were so wide open that he looked like an owl under a moonlit sky, and he was stuttering as he tried to find a way to explain his way out of his mistake.

Miguel took control. "Not a problem. I'm sorry. We'll make you a fresh sandwich and bag them separately." The cost of a bagel-and-cream-cheese sandwich for the shop was about thirty cents, all expenses factored in.

But no sooner had the words left Miguel's mouth than the mastodon shouted, "You should fire that fuckin' piece of shit! I'm Jewish and he's Palestinian, and he did this shit on purpose because I'm a Jew! You need to fire his ass now!"

Miguel immediately realized a couple of things: Firstly, this was not a service issue; rather, it was a dispute that had started millennia before bagels and lox. It was a volatile mix of a cultural schism, land rights, religious beliefs, and generational DNA. The Hatfields and McCoys had nothing on this squabble. If the animus was so easily ignited by a bagel with warm cream cheese, Miguel couldn't begin to imagine how short the fuse must be in the Middle East.

Secondly, this dude, this customer, was now stepping into Miguel's space, and although Miguel did not know where the belligerent motherfucker had been raised, he knew sure as hell that the mastodon didn't see *him* growing up in Spanish Harlem.

Miguel drew a line in the roasted pepper cream cheese and decided this was going to be his reenactment of the shoot-out at the O.K. Corral. As the situation unfolded in slow motion, he turned his head to see what Mo was doing and saw him cowering behind a shelving unit. All he could see was Mo's forehead and his eyes. Standing at six-foot-one, Miguel was just short of being eye to eye with the customer, but, possessing only half the body mass, he acknowledged he might be at a slight physical disadvantage. However, with his NYC streets' scrappiness backing him up, Miguel knew in his bones this situation was nothing compared to the daily encounters he had to win to move up and out of the shit he grew up in.

The mastodon's bellowing captured the attention of the other patrons in the shop, not to mention all of the staff. Everyone momentarily suspended their activities, including chewing, to focus on the main-event entertainment offered by Miguel and his opponent, and some may have begun laying bets on the outcome. In Miguel's mind, the customer was technically correct, but that did not excuse his aggressive behavior and targeted cultural disparagements toward Mo. Moreover, the dude had been offered a satisfactory solution to the issue but persisted in acting like an asshole. Lastly, he had physically and philosophically stepped into Miguel's domain, which Miguel loosely interpreted as a violation of his humanitarian protections afforded by the UN's Geneva Convention.

For Miguel, this confrontation presented a fantastic opportunity to exemplify the new rule of law that would be enforced at this shop. Miguel leaned forward so close to the customer that their noses were almost touching.

"I'm not firing this guy because you demand it. He apologized. I apologized. We offered to provide you with a fresh bagel-and-cream-cheese sandwich. And you still feel that acting like an asshole is warranted."

By now the patrons had put their food and utensils down, and the employees dropped what they were doing to observe the exchange. The stage was set for the can of incoming whoop-ass.

Miguel continued, "So here's your new sandwich, in a separate bag, and it'll be the last one you buy in this shop. Now get the fuck out of here. That's right. Walk the fuck out and don't ever come in here to buy anything, ever. I don't give a fuck where you go after today, but it won't be here. Get the fuck out."

Miguel saw the dude's shoulders droop, and his mouth was open but no words came out. He took his bagged sandwich and sheepishly strolled out. The mastodon had been de-tusked. The employees had smiles on their faces and collectively saw Miguel's defense of them as an uplifting turn of events.

Miguel hated the fact that the situation had escalated to this level, but felt it appropriate to aggressively counter what he felt was inappropriate, bullying behavior. He felt bad for Mo and the old Jewish guy, but he couldn't go back on what had just occurred. Miguel, Maria, and Esteban were not going to indulge offensive behavior—not from a customer or an employee. Adults had to behave according to how they would want to be treated, and the three of them were willing to sacrifice their investment to normalize civilized behavior.

As Miguel watched the Jewish dude walk away, he thought that, just like the streets, the bagel shop represented a roller coaster of cultures, ethnicities, and humanity, and although he silently hoped for the best, he mentally buckled up for a wild ride.

CHAPTER 5

In which Miguel faces a series of calamities, from a broken oven and forgotten suitcase to customers who don't want to pay their food bill.

It was two in the afternoon and Pepe had thrust the last batch of bagels for the day into the oven. In the first few weeks of running the shop, Esteban had noticed that large quantities of bagels had gone unsold at day's end, and while some were repackaged to sell at a discount the following day, most were either given to the employees to take home or were simply thrown out. Esteban and Maria began adjusting inventory levels based on daily sales to avoid the waste.

On this particular Saturday, Miguel had volunteered to close the shop. He was running on fumes after having completed his weekly eight-to-six, Monday-through-Friday corporate gerbil-on-the-wheel gig, and had been on his feet at the bagel shop since early morning.

Pepe popped out of the kitchen and tentatively approached Miguel. "Jefe, the oven stopped working."

Miguel instinctively knew this was not good news, but it took him time to process the development, as if he were experiencing a stroke. His response was uncharacteristically inane: "What does that mean, Pepe?"

"It means we can't make bagels, and we have to fix the machine as soon as possible because tomorrow is Sunday and we have to make a lot of bagels. We have to call the guys that fix the oven. The number is in the office."

Miguel snapped back into consciousness and realized his plans for kicking back on a Saturday night had hit a significant roadblock. It was now two thirty p.m. He called Maria and Esteban to tell them they had a problem with the oven. Losing commercial and retail sales on a Sunday was a sobering problem that Miguel had to solve with a degree of urgency.

"Hi. Loven Oven? Yeah. It's Miguel at the bagel shop at 4233 Warnock, and we have a problem. The oven is not working and we need to get this fixed as quickly as possible."

He hung up the phone. Help was on its way.

Since his early teens, Miguel had demonstrated uncanny ninja skills and uniquely possessed not nine, but ten symbolic "cat" lives that allowed him to navigate out of almost any challenging situation. The oven failure was not unlike other adverse situations that he had overcome.

He reflected on a time when he was working for a prominent ad agency in south Florida. Miguel had positioned himself to be the young corporate Turk who would accomplish much and overcome anything, and by simply outworking everyone else, he earned that status. He came into the office earlier and stayed longer. On a daily basis, he greeted his supervisors with a smile and a demitasse of Cuban cafecito. He gained the confidence of upper management, and as a result was directed to lead a meeting with one of the company's largest clients, based in California—one that happened to be a Fortune 100 company. He meticulously prepared for the meeting, focusing on every detail, no matter how small, to ensure its success.

His flight was scheduled to depart Miami International at four p.m., and during the day he would only have to get to the airport about forty-five minutes before takeoff. He reasoned that by leaving at three p.m. for his four p.m. flight, he would arrive at the airport with time to spare to deal with some paperwork for a couple of other clients. After all, the airport was only fifteen minutes away "as the crow flies." However, Miguel had just recently relocated to Miami and was not yet fully conversant with the chaotic traffic patterns and vehicular overcrowding that the city graciously provides.

Miguel left the office at three, threw his suitcase in the trunk of his Honda Civic, revved up its lawn mower engine, peeled out of the sand and dirt parking area, and abruptly confronted a concerning sea of red brake lights. As he scoured the horizon, he felt he did not need to panic. But this troubling development led Miguel to consider the possibility that he might miss his flight. He exited the highway as soon as he could and drove through nearby neighborhood streets, hoping to find an unencumbered road. He knew he was in the proximity of the airport and commandeered the Honda onto streets that looked like they might lead there. He was relieved when his rambling eventually led him to an airport service road connecting to a parking lot.

He looked at his watch. Three thirty. Thirty

minutes to get to the gate and onto his flight. With his heart banging in his chest and his carotid arteries pulsating, he arrived at his window seat with a scant five minutes to spare, and proceeded to congratulate himself on his resilience. As the plane pushed back from the gate, Miguel stopped sweating. He settled in for the long hop to LA and a meeting he would absolutely crush. Then a frozen expression gripped his face and beads of sweat once again collected on his brow. His brown suitcase remained in the trunk of his car. "My suitcase," gasped Miguel under his breath. "I left my fucking suitcase in the car. How the fuck could I have forgotten my suitcase? Unbelievable. I'm fucked."

Miguel's flight would arrive in LA around eight thirty in the evening, and the meeting was scheduled for nine the following morning. He had left behind his business attire, a pair of shoes, another set of casual clothes, and a toothbrush. He calmed his mind. He had a sliver of functional time to figure this out. Assuming retail shops were not a solution, what then?

When Miguel arrived at the Biltmore Hotel, he jumped out of the cab and immediately looked for a valet. He chose a valet over a hotel concierge because Miguel's experience provided him with the insight that valets could operate in a gray area where money carried significant influence. Miguel pinpointed the lead valet and approached him with a plan—and a few bills.

Seasoned valets are empathetic and professionally adept at recognizing someone with a dilemma. "What's up, man? How can I help you, sir?"

Do I look that obviously desperate? thought Miguel. "I sure hope so, dude. So, here's the deal. I left my suitcase in the car back in Miami, and I have a meeting tomorrow at nine. My business clothes are in that suitcase. I can get by with my khakis and penny loafers, but I need a tie and a sports jacket."

The boss valet smiled. "Bo! You got a second?" Bo was a security guard, an older man who was conversing with a hotel employee. As Bo sauntered over, Miguel assessed that he carried some authority. Bo greeted Miguel, then turned his attention to the valet. "What's up, Tom?"

"Bo, this guy needs some assistance, and I thought you might be able to help him. Bo is our head of security."

Miguel repeated his story.

Bo appeared amused. "Son, it looks like you're in a tight spot."

"Look, how about the hotel restaurant? Would they have any jackets? I know it's late, but are there any menswear stores open?"

Bo said, "The restaurant has a nasty spare jacket and tie, but I think they do it on purpose to humiliate the people who don't stick to the dress code. You won't find a local menswear store open until tomorrow. Tell me—what is your jacket size?"

"Forty-four long."

"Forty-four long? I think I can help you out. Follow me."

As he walked off with Bo, Miguel nodded at the valet and slipped him a twenty. Bo walked Miguel through a door that revealed the hotel security locker room. "You're in luck. We just got an order of jackets for security the other day, and I haven't had a chance to distribute all of them."

Miguel didn't understand the point of this exercise—he wasn't going to be able to wear a sports jacket with a Biltmore Hotel security badge embroidered on the front left pocket, like Bo was wearing.

"I have some that haven't been sent out to get embroidered yet. I mean, you certainly don't want this shit on your jacket."

Miguel vigorously shook his head, agreeing with him.

"You're good with navy blue, right, 'cause that's the only color available."

"Fuck yeah, Bo!" Miguel enthusiastically slipped on the jacket, and it fit like a glove.

"You think you can get by with this tie?" asked Bo, handing Miguel one of his standard work ties.

"Hell yes, Bo!" He handed Bo a fifty, which was gratefully received.

By ten the next morning the client had approved Miguel's meticulously written proposal.

"Jefe. JEFE!"

Emil, the gigolo mascot of the bagel shop, snapped Miguel out of his reverie.

"Jefe. Dos people have been here for una hora and they're leaving. Dey haven't paid for their food. Dey has been in store before and no paid."

"What did they order?"

"One number four sandwich, one bagel with lox and scallion cream cheese, four empanadas, two cafés con leche, a rice pudding, and a tres leches."

Miguel parked himself by the coffee station near the entrance to the shop. The couple casually got up from the table and made their way to the door. Miguel looked at Emil for confirmation that they had not paid for their meal. Emil signaled that they hadn't.

Miguel blocked the exit. "Excuse me for interrupting, folks. My name is Miguel, and I am the owner of the store. I wanted to ask you if you enjoyed the food today."

Miguel was duly informed that the food was excellent and that the bagel shop was one of their go-to places for good deli food. Miguel thanked them, then said, "I think you may have forgotten to pay for your meals."

Feigning surprise, the male customer responded by saying, "What? Of course we paid for the food."

"No, no. We absolutely paid for our food," interjected his companion.

"Frankly, I am offended that you are asking us this. If you don't mind, please move over." The man tried to push his way past Miguel.

Miguel resorted to his best Clint Eastwood impression. "I'll gladly move when you pay your bill." He threw the bolt on the door. "I am reliably informed you've done this before and got away with it. It ain't happening again."

"You can't do this!" yelled the woman. "You need to move over and let us leave!"

At that moment, another customer, who was a regular, motioned to Miguel that he'd like to leave. Miguel stepped aside and opened the door enough to allow the customer to squeeze through. "Thanks, Jimmy. See you tomorrow."

"You bet, Miguel. Good luck with this."

Miguel relocked the door. "I'm not unlocking this door until you pay. Could you just go take care of this, please?"

"You either let us out of this fucking place or I'm going to call the cops, right now. Where's your phone?"

Miguel, all the while maintaining an irritatingly satisfied milquetoast demeanor, said, "Lady, call the cops. Do us all a favor and call the cops. You are embarrassing my customers and my staff, who'd rather not witness your antics." He paused and then said, "And you are embarrassing yourselves, fancy dress and all." He continued, "Look, here's the deal: I am not going to let either of you leave, *and* I'm going to let you call the cops. In fact, here's the phone number for the police. Please, call the cops, and they can see the video for themselves." Miguel pointed to cameras installed in the ceiling. "But just remember, I'm doing you two a favor by NOT calling the cops."

Miguel turned to Emil. "Emil—you got your phone ready to call the police?"

"Sí, jefe." Emil lifted his right hand to make the point.

"Do you really want to call the cops? C'mon. Just take care of this and go. It'll be our little secret. You can even pay with a credit card, since the bill is seventy-five dollars, which happens to include a gracious twenty-five percent tip."

The agitated male customer stepped forward. "Listen, motherfucker! Get out of the fuck—"

During the exchange, Emil had alerted a couple of the staff that these people might pose trouble, and when they heard the customer say "Listen, motherfucker," they came forward from behind the counter. The male customer's eyes fully dilated when he took note of the movement of two employees the size of walruses, and he discontinued his speech mid-sentence and submissively proceeded to the cashier to settle the bill. Silence was restored. Miguel unlocked the door, and as the couple departed, he wished them well and advised them that they were no longer welcome at his store.

Emil was relieved at the innocuous conclusion of this episode, but reinforced his commitment to back Miguel up. "Jefe, we were ready to go! All of us!"

Miguel was genuinely impressed with the bravado

demonstrated by Emil and the other two employees, but he could not afford to dwell on that sentiment because he now had to pivot his ninja skills to resolving another problem: repairing the oven. It was four p.m., closing time, and Loven Oven was not going to arrive until six p.m.

Emil asked, "Jefe, do ju want me to stay, or ju gonna stay until de oven is fix?"

"No, Emil. Thank you. Go home. I am staying."

"Gracias, jefe. De udder owners would always make me or Pepe stay until dey fix de oven, and dey would go a la casa."

The few remaining customers and employees departed, leaving Miguel by himself to wait for the Loven Oven crew. While he waited, he recalled the unusual forewarning another restaurateur had offered him—*the money you make in the restaurant business is blood money*—Miguel had originally flinched at the comment. *If you want to be successful, the restaurant will consume your life. You have to be there all the time. You can't trust anyone. Not even people that work for you. Employees steal if you're not there. It is blood money. Your blood.*

That man knew what he was talking about. Holidays for the Cuban clan would never be the same now that they had taken custody of the bagel shop, because it was open 365 days a year, holidays and all.

Loven Oven showed up at six and spent the next five hours—of which three were probably unnecessary—repairing the oven. Once the oven was tested and declared operational, the crew left. Miguel closed up and had just enough time to go home, take a shower, and get some sleep; he had to be back at the shop the next morning at eight a.m., because he was determined to collect his blood money.

CHAPTER 6

In which a Bruce Lee imitation is thwarted, and what sounds like the voice of God thunders in a certain neighborhood in Harlem late at night where Noel's dad's new Caddy attracts unwelcome attention.

Living in NYC means possessing survival skills comprised of Olympic-caliber mental agility and physical strength, which, together, permit the outwitting of or physically beating the shit out of an enemy, competitor, or both—traits any person would undoubtedly utilize in many professional and personal circumstances in life. However, New York City is also an environment that enriches the curious mind and spirit, providing an intoxicating opportunity to explore the cultural, culinary, and architectural wonders that the world has to offer. This world landscape presented an explorer's opportunity for a young and impressionable Miguel, which he embraced eagerly.

Miguel was lucky enough to have had parents with the foresight to actively advocate for their son's educational freedom and also exploit the benefits associated with attending an elite (and very expensive) private school located on the Upper East Side of Manhattan. But while he deftly made his way into the upper echelons of society through his ability to make friends at school, Miguel still had to walk between the raindrops that fell between a Ralph Lauren store and the pages of a JCPenney catalog, or a Zabar's and a bodega.

Fortunately, Miguel had the nimbleness of mind to straddle two identities, because on one day he felt like a typical sewer rat, running around the streets of Spanish Harlem playing stickball and basketball, while on another he was hanging out in the privileged nests of his teenage friends living either in the upper-crust arrogance ("I want you to know that I am rich, and you're not") of the Upper East Side or in the disingenuous affectations ("I have so much money that I camouflage my uncompromising elitism by creating a delusional utopia in which my attire of vintage rags obscures my narcissistic financial superiority while I insincerely feign to be every other New Yorker's equal externally—but not really") of those with postal codes on the Upper West Side of Manhattan. Of course, Miguel did not know at the time how this colorful cultural intersection was a supreme gift that contributed to his intellectual evolution.

At the high school of the rich and famous, one late-spring day, Professor Rothenberg was writing the chemistry final exam questions on the blackboard, and the students were copying them into their notebooks, when he began to slowly tilt backwards. Then he began to flail furiously as if both arms were wind turbines spinning in a forty-mile-an-hour wind, in an attempt to regain his balance. He resorted to grabbing the top of the blackboard with his right hand to pull himself erect. It wasn't the first time the students had witnessed their teacher's antics, and they were not surprised. The professor had previously satisfied the students' curiosity regarding his "balancing acts" when he had described his colorful college experiences at the State University of New York, wherein he couldn't understand how he had been able to graduate college, much less achieve his doctorate degree in chemistry, because he had been stoned every day at school. His revealing and honest biographical testimony, coupled with his endearing personality, made Professor Rothenberg a favorite teacher amongst the majority of the student body.

It was also entertainingly obvious to students that Professor Rothenberg lived true to his tales, and he looked the part. He had a head of hair that looked like it had just experienced a kerfuffle, an impressively shaggy beard, and a mustache that served as a partial homage to Albert Einstein. His fashion choices also remained true to the stereotype: a herringbone tweed suit jacket with a woolen vest (except during the summer, when his fall and winter ensemble was replaced by seersucker) and, for added eccentricity, a classic vintage pocket watch. The outfit was completed with tan khakis and a pair of counterculture Earth shoes.

Earth shoes were designed by a Danish yoga instructor and shoe designer by the name of Anna Kalso, and their distinguishing feature is something called a Negative Heel Technology sole, which is much thinner in the heel than it is in the front of the shoe and is, in theory, supposed to make a person feel like they are walking in sand. Although Professor Rothenberg was up on his chemistry, he failed to grasp the physics of wearing such a shoe, which contributed to his loss of balance.

The class was relieved that Professor Rothenberg had avoided an unplanned ass plant and, as such, had only momentarily distracted them from focusing on the exam questions.

Miguel excelled at chemistry but nonetheless was getting annoyed with the classmate in front of him. Timothy Adler was the son of a CEO of a prominent multinational corporation who was absent in person and spirit for most of Tim's life. Tim had become a heroin addict by the time he was fifteen years old. The addiction had resulted in a change of address from an opulent brownstone located in the mid-sixties between Lexington and Third avenues to a bleak temporary residence at a prominent drug rehabilitation facility for troubled teens near Hell's Kitchen on the west side of Manhattan. After Tim progressed through recovery and was cleared to be released, his parents (or rather, his mother) proceeded to apply to multiple private high schools in the borough in the hope that proper academics and social interaction would help acclimate Tim to a normal and drugless lifestyle. The school that accepted Tim did so after receiving a blank check, much to the joy of the headmaster but to the dismay of the new pupil.

Without knowing his past travails, anyone who interacted with Tim would not have suspected the level of psychological turmoil he had experienced as a youth. He had a personality that was vibrant, fun, and engaging, never spoke ill of anyone, and treated everyone respectfully, and all of the students had happily welcomed him.

"Tim ... what the fuck are you doing?" whispered Miguel as Professor Rothenberg was looking down at his notes.

Tim whispered back to Miguel through one side of his mouth, without turning around: "Dude, check in my right pocket."

Miguel reached across the desk into the right pocket of Tim's purple velvet sports jacket, which featured gold accents on the lapels and side pockets, and resembled something that could have been left behind in a dressing room by the Grateful Dead. He was hoping that whatever it was Tim had secreted in his pocket, it had nothing to do with the exam. It didn't. The object had a circumference of about an inch, and was about ten inches long. It reminded Miguel of when he was in grade school and his mother had given him a pencil case designed to look like a large No. 2 pencil. Or maybe, because it was the last exam before the summer break, it could be a Roman candle.

Miguel whispered, "Tim, what the hell is this?"

"Take it out," responded Tim.

Miguel excavated the large cylindrical shape and was surprised to see it wasn't, as he had originally suspected, either a pencil case or a firecracker. It looked like a giant joint.

"Tim—is this what it looks like?"

This time, Tim took the opportunity to gleefully fully turn around, showcasing a broad shit-eating grin. "It is exactly that."

Apparently, Tim had made use of a huge rolling paper included as a promotional item in a Cheech and Chong album titled *Big Bambú*.

It was then that Professor Rothenberg noticed the semi-muted exchange between Tim and Miguel and put his hands on the desk to help secure his equilibrium long enough to ask, "Hey, guys, what's going on back there?"

Miguel quickly deposited the item into Tim's pocket, hoping an investigation wouldn't lead to an accusation of cheating. However, most inexplicably, Miguel happily blurted out, "Professor Rothenberg ... you should see what Tim has in his pocket!"

Tim began laughing under his breath, because he felt sure that Professor Rothenberg, being the legendary stoner he declared himself to be and teaching in a progressive liberal school, would just tell him not to interrupt the exam with stupid jokes. Instead, curiosity got the better of Professor Rothenberg. "Well, Tim, why don't you share what you have hidden in your pocket with the rest of class."

Tim enthusiastically pulled out his giant joint and held it above his head like the sword of a conquering medieval knight. The sight elicited gasps and guffaws. Despite himself, Rothenberg maintained decorum. "Is that what I think it is, Timothy?"

"Indeed it is, professor. I dropped a whole ounce of pot into the *Big Bambú* rolling paper."

"So, Tim, where are we going after the exam?" the professor asked gleefully.

Once liberated from the classroom, select friends, along with Tim, Miguel, and the professor, gathered at the iconic Central Park fountain, where the scent of pot permeated the air and which was ground zero in attracting Frisbee players, roller skaters, stoners, and other free spirits in the city. It was the ultimate safe harbor for them to light up the tiki torch of a joint Tim had constructed. It made the rounds just as a close friend of Miguel's magically appeared through the haze. It was Noel Abramowitz, a senior on the basketball team with Miguel. Noel was hard to miss. He measured six-foot-five and had exceptionally long arms, a nose that stretched into another zip code, and a perm he thought complemented his naturally light-colored hair.

"Hey, Miguel. We're on for tonight, right?"

"Of course we are!" exclaimed Miguel.

"And my dad lent me the car for tonight."

"Your dad let you have his Caddy? The Seville?"

"Yes, sir!"

"The one he just got this year?"

"Yupper," confirmed Noel as Miguel excitedly reacted with a reenactment of a boxer furiously landing body blows on his opponent. The group, having done as much damage to the joint as was humanly possible, happily bid each other farewell with this initiation into the summer holidays.

As they walked through Central Park, Noel and Miguel caught sight of a group of five kids who attended a rival private high school, which, due to a premium on local real estate, also used Central Park for gym classes and a variety of other activities.

"Look at those assholes." Miguel had stopped to reconnoiter the group at about fifty yards' distance. "I can't stand those guys."

"Looks like they might feel the same way about us," commented a wary Noel.

Miguel did not appear to be concerned about their response. He thought himself a tough dude from Spanish Harlem, and he was experiencing a testosterone rush and bravado courtesy of Tim's pot.

"Miguel—stop, dude. We have dates tonight. We can't risk getting into a fucking fight now. Plus, we're only two guys and they've got five."

What Noel didn't know was that Miguel was carrying a secret weapon that would give them a considerable advantage in a fight—a nunchaku that Miguel had tucked away under his belt on his lower back. The martial arts weapon, which was also used for training in addition to combat, was made popular by Bruce Lee in *Enter the Dragon*, the movie that inspired legions of fans and cemented his legend around the world as a kung fu master.

Over the course of several months, Miguel had taught himself how to use the nunchaku he had purchased illegally from a small shop located in the bowels of Chinatown, which sold a wide range of illegal martial arts weapons. Eschewing professional lessons, Miguel opted to reenact every detail of Bruce Lee's kung fu film sequences that showcased him using a nunchaku, which also included his mimicking Lee's signature "ki-ai" when he engaged in a fight. (Screaming "ki-ai" is designed to intimidate opponents, but more importantly allows the body to exhale useless carbon dioxide and resupply it with a fresh delivery of needed oxygen.)

"Look what I got, Noel." Miguel pulled out the nunchaku as they neared the other group.

"Nunchucks? You have nunchucks? You brought those to school?"

"Yeah, why not?"

"Because you're not supposed to bring weapons to school. You know that."

"It's not a big deal. And I'm glad I did bring them with me today, now that we ran into these assholes."

"Are you fucking with me, dude? I don't want to get into a fucking fight. I don't fight for no reason, but I love for any reason, and I would love to go shoot some hoops right now."

"Well, my man, don't worry. We are going to go right away to shoot hoops, because once these jerks see the Bruce Lee shit I do with my sticks, they'll fucking bolt. Watch this."

Noel tentatively stepped aside as Miguel began yelling at the rival group, "Hey, assholes …"

The rivals held their ground as Miguel demonstrated his nunchaku routine, accompanied by a "ki-ai" sound effect that sounded like a cross between a guttural cackle and a coughing fit from someone suffering from COPD. Noel anxiously looked about as Miguel, following his routine, maintained the classic nunchaku attack stance, deadly Bruce Lee stare included.

The rival kids appeared perplexed, then amused, as they applauded in unison.

"I think they're making fun of you, Miguel," offered a stoic Noel.

Miguel was not to be deterred. "C'mon, motherfuckers! Come git some of this!"

Miguel and Noel did not stop running for what felt like a mile, until they arrived in a safe harbor on school grounds.

"I thought"—*wheeze, gasp, wheeze, cough, gasp, wheeze*—"I thought"—*gasp*—"that they were going to skip when they saw your nunchucks." *Wheeze.* "Why'd we run?" *Cough, cough.* Noel was bent over with his hands on his knees and desperately urging his lungs to mine for oxygen.

"Those guys are fucking crazy," responded Miguel, who was also bent over and unable to control the flow he spit onto the sidewalk as he was trying to breathe. "I'm not fighting any fuckers that start running at me to take on nunchucks. That's nuts."

"And the little guy out front. He was only like five feet tall. Those are the guys I'm most afraid of. Those little guys are like pit bulls. They feel no pain."

"Yeah. No way. Angry short man? He's got nothing to lose. No way, Jose. Let's go play some ball before we have to get ready, Noel."

. . .

Noel's family lived in a swanky apartment building located on 76th and Riverside Drive. It was such an exclusive property that even the doormen behaved as if their generational bloodlines stemmed from having served centuries of aristocracy. However, it was also right across the street from a public space that housed two basketball courts and stone chess tables. It was a hangout for grifters, drug dealers, and gamblers, who plied their trade against a backdrop of incessant basketball thumping.

Miguel and Noel often practiced and communed with other players, mostly Black with a sprinkling of white (more like a dash than a sprinkle), and street thugs who used the park as a second home and business address. Noel and Miguel understood that improving their game meant leaving behind the homogenous confines of the Upper East Side and the predominantly white guys who couldn't jump or trash-talk. It meant playing pickup games with the "brothers."

As Miguel and Noel waited their turn for a game, a Black guy sprinted by them at what seemed to be the speed of a cheetah. "Holy shit! Did you see that? I don't think his feet were even touching the ground," exclaimed Noel as he felt the faint effect of wind that was generated by the runner.

Miguel was also caught by surprise. "Fucking guy was a blur, bro. He ran by us in half a second. Amazing."

"He must be chasing somebody, or he stole something."

Minutes later, the speedster returned carrying a ten-speed racing bike on his shoulder, and a young white kid ran up to him, profusely thanking him and hugging him. Miguel and Noel were mystified by what they had just witnessed until they overheard another player waiting to get on the court.

"Man, that dude is a safety for the Kansas City Chiefs. He's from this area, so he comes back after football season and hangs out around here for a couple weeks."

The incident impressed Miguel. "Damn amazing. He caught up to a guy that rode off with that kid's bike? And brought it back to him? Great shit. I would hate to be chased by that dude on a football field."

Noel looked thoughtful. "So that's how fast professional football players are? Damn. It's like having superpowers."

After reaching the eleven-point winner-take-all score in their version of five-on-five street basketball, the players on the winning team stayed on the court and waited to face new opponents.

Noel dug an elbow into Miguel's side. "Let's go. The game's over. We have the court now. Who else is playing with us?"

The two friends knew a pretty decent ensemble of players would be needed to unseat the current winning team, which was comprised of two Division 1 college players—one from Wake Forest University and the other from the University of Massachusetts. But then Magnus announced he'd be siding with Miguel and Noel. "Yo, niggas! Let's play! I'm with you two white boys!"

Magnus was considered a street basketball legend in his own right and was the unofficial mascot of the courts. He stood about five-foot-seven and was a coal-colored guy with arms that were so long his hands dangled below his knees, making him a dribbling savant worthy of Harlem Globetrotter status. Because of the short distance between his hands and the court floor, the basketball barely needed to bounce up above his ankles before it touched his hands, making it practically impossible to steal a ball from him. He was also a prolific long-distance shooter, a drunk, and a heroin addict. He would often show up to play basketball with bloodshot eyes, off-balance, slurring his speech, and with a half-smoked cigarette stored above one of his earflaps. No matter his level of impairment, Magnus would always light up the court, while constantly uttering an endless stream of trash talk.

As they stepped onto the court to quickly warm up, Miguel engaged Magnus in conversation to determine how fucked-up he was. It was still early enough in the day, and a short exchange with Magnus told Miguel he was court-worthy. Miguel wasn't the only one excited to see Magnus put on a show, and Magnus did not disappoint, nailing shots from otherworldly sections of the court and making magical passes to his teammates for easy layups. He dribbled circles around the other team, to the obvious embarrassment of the Division 1 college players. Miguel and Noel won four consecutive games with Magnus, and then decided it was time to leave and get cleaned up for their social escapades with two very pretty ladies.

It was also time for Magnus to start drinking heavily.

It was six p.m. when, from his apartment window, Miguel spotted Noel double-parked down the street in a brand-new Cadillac Seville. Noel was hard to miss—a white dude in a Caddy in Spanish Harlem. The car could easily have been mistaken for a pimp's car if people didn't bother to look closely at the white-as-chalk driver. Miguel understandably hustled down to the street, urging Noel to quickly vacate the neighborhood.

"You ready? Let's go pick up the girls. They're waiting for us at Alicia's house."

To some degree Noel was a stranger in a strange land, and as he drove through blocks upon blocks of dilapidated tenement buildings, he could not help noticing the panoply of shirts, pants, socks, and underwear that had been hung out to dry on a maze of laundry lines that extended across to other buildings. Alternatively, clothes were draped over fire escapes as if they were the national flags of foreign countries. He stopped at a light to witness throngs of people hanging out on the stoops and in the streets due to the stifling heat or to escape the crush of eight people jammed into a one-bedroom apartment.

"Holy shit, Miguel. Are we safe around here?"

Miguel chuckled. "My man, if you were by yourself, you'd probably be walking around carrying just a hubcap in your hands."

As they drove along, Miguel grimly reflected that while he was able to visit the exclusive bastions of his pedigreed friends, they never traveled to his neighborhood to visit him.

"Hurry up. Just slide the car into the hydrant space."

Noel brought the luxury-on-wheels to a halt on 81st Street, just off Central Park West and alongside the world-famous Museum of Natural History.

"Stay right here, Noel. I'll be right back with Alicia and Monica." Miguel jumped out of the car and requested permission from the doorman to enter the exclusive domain of the classic Beresford, where Alicia lived. After a brief conversation, Miguel returned to the car. He had been told to wait while the doorman notified Ms. Alicia Daniels that her guests had arrived. Ten minutes later, Noel and Miguel greeted both girls, and they departed for the party in Long Island. "We got forty-five minutes to get there, so we have to move," Miguel said.

The party was hosted by Alicia's cousin, and the estate provided ample evidence of generational wealth. Miguel thought he might run into the ghost of the Great Gatsby. At eleven p.m. the couples left the party and scampered to the car. Noel only had until midnight to get the car home safely.

"Fastest way home is to cut across 125th Street after the Triborough, go to Riverside Drive, and go down through there." Miguel knew they were headed into a "no-go zone" for white people, but with the restrictive timeline to deliver the car, he felt he was left with no other option.

"Noel, don't stop at any red lights. Just make sure other cars aren't coming and keep driving through."

"What are you talking about, Miguel? I don't want to get a ticket."

"Noel—don't act brain-dead. There are no police cars up here. Trust me. This is not your neighborhood. They don't have cop cars here or even where I live. So just keep driving and don't stop," he pleaded.

"Dude, what are you talking about? There's barely anyone on the streets."

Miguel acknowledged that there were few people on the streets, but he also recognized that it was close to midnight, and the people who were wandering around Harlem at this time were people he did not want to meet. They had almost exited Black Harlem when the engine started to sputter, and soon quit altogether. The Caddy hauntingly came to a dead stop. Only a few seconds ticked by before the car drew the attention of a small block party that had congregated in front of an all-night convenience store, which, thanks to the steel rods lacing the front window, looked more like a military outpost.

"What the fuuucckk?" Noel flaccidly commented as the blood seemed to drain from his face. Miguel looked at the blank expressions of their dates as Noel added a succinct "We're so fucked."

Miguel insisted, "Shit. This isn't good, but let's see how we can get out of this. Try starting the car again, Noel."

Noel turned the key as beads of sweat formed on his forehead and upper lip.

"Look at what we got here! A fucking Caddy with a bunch of white kids. Jerome! Did you drive a Caddy when you were a kid?"

"Nigga, I don't even know who my daddy is," responded Jerome, as he doubled over laughing while pointing at the car.

Miguel shook Noel's shoulder. "Noel! Noel, goddammit!"

"The car won't start. Now what? We need to call for a tow."

"Miguel … where are we?" whispered Alicia as she locked her door. "Why are we stopping here?"

Miguel turned to the ladies, who were trying to shrink down in the back seat. "Stay put." Then, "Let's see if there's a phone we can use in the store."

As Noel and Miguel cautiously stepped out of the car, a few members of the crowd moved as if to confront them. Just then, an imposing Black man, who had lowered his head to step out of the convenience shop, exclaimed with a commanding voice, "Where you fools going?" No one inched forward.

Big Voice approached the Caddy. "Dey know better dan to fuck wid me because I take care of da boss in dis neighborhood, and he takes care of me." He stared at Noel and Miguel. "What de fuck are you crackers doing 'round here? Yous fuckin' crazy? Or yous just a couple of dumbass white boys and girls?"

Miguel found his voice. "Well, sir, I just wanna say, just for the record, I'm not white. I'm actually Cuban and live in Spanish Harlem."

A voice from the chorus in back said, "So, you a spic, then? You don' look like a spic. You look like a white boy. I bet you don' even know how to speaki de ekspañol." Out of a sense of respect (but more fear than respect), Miguel nodded his head so as not to disagree with the comment, but realized that breaking out in fluent Spanish might be a sign of disrespect.

"But den you should know better than bringin' your friends around here!" admonished the tall Black man. "Your car crapped out, son?"

Noel rigidly responded, "Yes sir, sir."

"How da fuck can this car crap out? It's a fuckin' Caddy," he said, as Noel shrugged his shoulders.

"Relax, son. I'm not gonna do anything to you guys 'cept hep yous. I would say les open de hood, but I don' know shit about cars. Never had one. Never want one. Don't wanna be driving around and have the shit break down in neighborhoods like this."

Despite Big Voice's assurance, Miguel and Noel did their best to impersonate utility poles.

"You people stay here, and I gonna go inside and call you a tow truck. It's a friend of mine, and he'll come lickety-split as long as he ain't fuckin' one a his nine girlfriends. Plus, yous knows dat yous ain't gettin' any tow trucks up here unless it's a tow truck brother. Ain't no white tow trucks comin' up here, even to tow white people."

Big Voice turned to the spectators. "And you assholes stay da fuck put! Ya unnerstan'! Don't fuckin' go near dem!" He turned to the friends. "I be right back!"

"Who was that? Are we going to be alright?" asked Alicia, anxiously sinking into the back seat with her friend.

"I'm pretty sure that's who owns the convenience shop. Did you hear that voice?" responded Miguel. "It sounded like the voice of God—or doom."

Big Voice wasn't gone for long. "Well, my buddy ain't fuckin' no one, so he figured he'll make some drinkin' money. Said he's only a mile away and should be here in fifteen minutes. If ya'll want someding to eat, come inside and git someding. You"—he pointed at Noel—"come inside and pick some stuff out for you and your friends, and you"—he pointed at Miguel—"stay out here with the girls and the car."

Noel returned within five minutes and distributed some chips and sodas. "Dude, you should have seen the inside of the shop. It looked like a bomb shelter. There were Plexiglas dividers on the front counter between the customer and the cash register, and there was this little opening where you slid your money in to pay and get your change."

At that moment, the tow truck pulled up and a jumpy little Black guy bounced out of the truck. "Let me guess … wait … one more second … Yeah, tha's it! Yous the white people I'm supposed to tow. You motherfuckers must be crazy."

"OK, Mickey. Tha's enough, son. Get to work and get these fine young folks outta here." Big Voice had quietly come out of his shop to speak to Mickey, while simultaneously keeping his eyes on the convenience shop street flies.

The Caddy was soon hooked up. Ismael flashed a wide grin and said, "You guys are set. Go wid God."

Miguel and Noel thanked him profusely. Then Alicia spoke up to address the fact that they hadn't been introduced and asked what his name was.

"My name is Ismael," he responded proudly, and when Miguel and Noel offered him some money for his help, he waved his hands and humbly declined.

"No, no, no. Dat's not necessary. Not at all."

"But you saved our asses tonight, Ismael. We really appreciate it."

"I unnestan'. I unnestan'. But yous gotta do what's right because God watches over me. And he obviously watches over yous as well. So I hope yous learned somedin' and nex' time do something right fo' someone else. Tha's all. Is not complicated. Is simple."

The four crammed into the front seat of the tow truck, which looked like it might need a tow itself in the not-to-distant future, hoping it would last long enough to get them home. As it started to rumble down the street, they waved goodbye to Ismael and his street gang and sat quietly reflecting on the events that had just transpired. Miguel thought out loud, "We hit the lottery. Finding a guy like Ismael at midnight, and in Harlem, was a one-in-a-thousand encounter, and I need to make sure not to put myself in a position where I'm playing those odds. Lesson thankfully learned."

After twenty minutes had passed, Alicia broke the silence by blurting out, "I'm hungry!"

"I'm hungry too, but it's two in the morning. Where are we gonna find a place to eat?" said Miguel.

Noel came to life. "H&H Bagels! It's on the way to the garage where we're dropping off the car, and it's open twenty-four seven. Mickey, you hungry?"

"I'm always hungry, my man!"

"You like bagels?" asked Alicia.

"Yea. I like the onyun ones. Those are my favorite."

"Then you are in for a treat, my friend. We're only minutes away."

The tow truck pulled to the curb outside H&H Bagels and Miguel hurried inside. He returned with two armfuls of bagels. "Here's a bag of bagels for you, and I put in two tubs of cream cheese as well. Give half of these to Ismael, OK? Make sure he gets them."

"Yeah, yeah, I got you. Thanks, man."

They were soon in Noel's kitchen, doing their best not to disturb the peace. *Not a bad night after all*, thought Miguel, *and this bagel tastes pretty good.*

CHAPTER 7

In which immersions into American culture include pilgrimages of some hundreds of miles and a few city blocks, tall tales, and the Rockettes.

Onaydis and Rolando's ten-year-old 1963 Pontiac Bonneville rust bucket of an automobile was rumbling south on Interstate 95 for its annual pilgrimage to Miami Beach. Like birds flying south in the winter or salmon swimming upstream to revisit the birth streams of their chemical signature, every Fourth of July saw the start of a migration of Cubans who lived north of the 40th parallel to South Florida. Theirs was a spiritual quest for a faux Cuban dreamscape a mere ninety miles from Cuba.

During and immediately after the Cuban Revolution, Miami Beach and the surrounding Dade County communities were engulfed with newly arrived Cubans, many of whom chose to stay in South Florida because of the warm weather, palm trees, and cultural similarity to Cuba. Others, however, headed north to pursue the abundant job opportunities that could be found in the cold temperatures, towering skyscrapers, and shadow-lined streets that checkered the New York metropolitan tri-state area. The one degree of separation from friends and family grew into an annual tradition that involved a two- or three-week family convalescence in Little Havana and Miami Beach.

The summer driving exodus to South Florida (nobody ever flew) unsurprisingly spawned a kind of Greek mythic storytelling, given the Cuban proclivity for song and poetry. The writers of these mythological tales were mostly adult male Cubans who relished the opportunity to brag to their compadres about their magnificent driving skills that allowed them to break land-speed records for the twelve hundred miles to Miami Beach. The tales suggested these drivers were behind the wheel of a Ferrari competing in the 24 Hours of Le Mans, when in reality they were driving an ancient sedan with the windows down for the little relief a crossbreeze might offer.

The ones hell-bent on achieving an obnoxiously fictitious level of lore would brag about having made the trip from New York City to Miami Beach in an unprecedented nineteen hours, prescriptively articulating how they would switch drivers every six hours and would only stop for snacks, gas, and bathroom breaks—all happening at the same time, as if they were pulling into a NASCAR pit stop. Nineteen hours was scoffed at by others who said they could prove they made the trip in eighteen hours—highly dubious but not easy to disprove. What was incontrovertible was a Cuban's birthright to predict a new record drive time to Miami Beach in the next vacation season.

As the Fourth of July holiday approached and families began preparing for the trip, a familiar scene would play out in the Hispanic neighborhoods of

New Jersey. Neighbors would share dinner, as was common practice, and conversation would turn to the annual Cuban car rally to Miami. Following dinner, the men convened in the family room and, in between bellows of tobacco smoke, boasted about their driving prowess and how they'd make the trip in record time. The women repaired to the kitchen, where they relished the opportunity to rebut the falsehoods offered up by their male counterparts, a pastime that provided them with endless amusement.

"We made it down there last year in nineteen hours, and this year we are going to be there in eighteen hours, if not más rápido," exclaimed Jose to the other road warriors.

His wife overheard his claims and shouted, "Jose, what are you talking about!?" Her booming voice rattled the glasses in the kitchen cabinet.

"No, woman! What are *you* talking about? It was nineteen hours last year, and I will have us there in eighteen hours on this trip!" huffed Jose.

"Ay, Dios mio … it took us twenty-six hours to get there last year, Jose. Para de hablar mierda. Remember, you are not counting the several times we stopped to visit Pedro's South of the Border or Myrtle Beach, where we went to the boardwalk with the kids."

The men had become used to full-throated denials from their spouses, as none was spared, and out of respect waited for Jose's counterthrust. But none was to come. He stood defeated by his own incredulity, made worse when his wife pulled the rug from beneath his feet by proclaiming, "This year, we are staying overnight in a hotel. It's stupid to do that trip in one day. I don't even want to talk about it."

The women in the kitchen were roaring with laughter as Jose's wife described their travel plans, leaving her husband to wiggle on the hook. Beneath the repartee was the acknowledgment that Cuban women are strong, practical, and tactical, and enforcing the rules of the road was a natural extension of ruling the household.

And what everyone knew, of course, was that the states of Georgia and both Carolinas were anxious to dish out pure Southern hospitality in the form of speeding tickets, especially to Hispanics. Miraculously, it seemed *no one* was ever stopped by these Bible Belt police troopers and given speeding tickets—if anyone attested to being pulled over, it would invalidate their surreal driving claims. This was the Cuban northeast-to-southeast corridor version of the infamous coast-to-coast Gumball Rally. Eventually, boisterous claims of driving superiority became the domain of memory.

Also remembered was how Cuban parents and children would wake up at four in the morning to load up the car for their Chevy Chase to Wallyworld road trip. At the edge of dawn, everyone got out of bed and packed the car. At six a.m., the father would turn the ignition key and the engine would cough up a cloud of black smoke. As the engine warmed up, the neighborhood was treated to *pop-pop-pop* firecracker sounds emanating from the tailpipe as a morning wake-up alarm (thankfully not, this time, a drive-by shooting), a heralded esprit de corps trumpeting the commencement of the family's annual vacation. As Jose's wife had eloquently pointed out, most traveling families did not rush their road trip in pursuit of breakneck driving speeds, instead taking the time to nourish themselves with the sights and sounds the southeast had to offer, the most notable of which (at least to Cubans, who had a cultural affinity to the name Pedro) was the infamous but just as easily forgettable

Pedro's South of the Border tourist attraction.

Conveniently located and highly visible from the interstate, Pedro's South of the Border (formerly South of the Border Depot, which provided retail alcohol to dry counties in North Carolina) was and still is an iconic landmark exit that delineated the boundary between North and South Carolina and represented the halfway point between New York and Florida. Whether you were going north or south on Interstate 95, excruciatingly kitschy billboards starting sixty miles away extolled Pedro's fun-filled family activities, using fitting but horrible puns like "You Never Saw Sausage a Place," "You're Always a Weiner at Pedro's," and "Time for a Paws," accompanied by cheesy pseudo-Mexican artwork featuring Mexican peasants wearing large sombreros and strumming guitars.

After miles upon miles of billboards building anticipation, Pedro's suddenly appeared on the horizon, a striking monolith resembling Seattle's Space Needle and larger than the largest Bob's Big Boy statue—the Sombrero Observation Tower soars two hundred feet and is adorned with a huge, colorful sombrero. While parents had their reservations about stopping at an acknowledged tourist trap of the first rank, it was a rite of passage anointing a new generation's assimilation into America—including the families of Miguel and Maria and Esteban.

Another rite of passage was surviving almost literally a highway through hell. The climate in the southeast in July and August was a bayou medley of suffocating humidity and sweltering heat. Afternoon temperatures would hit ninety-five degrees, and cars and their occupants were exposed to blinding sunlight from a cloudless sky and the lava-esque heat rising from the pavement. The dizzying heat led one, in a heat-stroke-inspired state of delusion, to misinterpret the hazy horizon for a body of water or a sign of rain.

The delightful concoction of exhaust fumes and searing air enveloped all the passengers as Esteban, Maria, and their younger brother, Eduardo, wiped the perspiration from their eyes and peered out their open car window to see an inspiring sight: A beautifully slick, light-blue Oldsmobile 88 with tinted windows and New Jersey plates was effortlessly passing them.

"Oooh, that's a pretty color, but why are their windows so dark? And why aren't the windows open?" asked an innocent Maria.

"They should open their windows!" offered Eduardo.

"It must be REALLY HOT in there!" added Esteban, grateful for the tropical breeze that unsuccessfully cooled his perspiration and, unbeknownst to him, added to his dehydration.

Meanwhile, Rolando sat silently fantasizing about a cool respite as he admired the air-conditioned, state-of-the-art Oldsmobile 88 drifting off into the horizon like a cowboy riding off into the sunset, quietly deciding to not reveal to his kids that there was actually a way to travel in a car without losing five to ten pounds of water weight.

The oppressive travel conditions resulted in the unrelenting smells that heat creates with dry, parched throats and cracked lips, as if the family had been roaming the desert for days, blindly searching for an oasis. But the torturous heat did not deter any of the traveling Cuban families—they were accustomed to Caribbean heat.

The suffering will end, thought Esteban, *when we get to Florida, because we will be welcomed by the inviting blue waters of the Atlantic Ocean, accompanied by beach umbrellas and sixteen ounces of little nuggets of crushed ice drenched in crisp, refreshing Coca-Cola.*

"We've made it!" was the collective, exuberant outburst as they saw the "Welcome to Florida" sign at the northern border of the state.

"Tranquilos. No hemos llegado todavia," explained Onaydis.

"¿Por qué no, mami?" asked Maria.

"Because …" Onaydis spun through the radio signals, searching for a Spanish-language station in an attempt to reassure her restless tribe. "We haven't found a radio station from Miami yet. So we have a little bit more to go." Then reality set in: They had seven more anguished hours of driving before they would reach the shores of Miami Beach.

Unlike Maria and Eduardo, Esteban was motivated to avoid complaining about the remaining agonizing portion of the trip, thanks to a tradition his parents had established to commemorate their Miami Beach pilgrimage. Each year, the siblings received a gift upon their departure, and this year it was a particularly memorable one. Maria had received a new bathing suit, sandals, and swimming goggles; Eduardo, swimming goggles, a Frisbee, and an inflatable water board; and Esteban, a speargun with a small trident spear, a snorkel, a mask, and a pair of fins. Esteban was a huge fan of the popular TV show *Sea Hunt*. In his mind's eye, the star of *Sea Hunt*, Lloyd Bridges, asked him to come along on his ocean adventures.

Soon, to their relief and delight, they finally heard a Spanish song on the radio. It was the sign they had been waiting for, and as Onaydis started to sing along with a Tito Puente salsa hit, their excitement grew exponentially because they knew they were getting close. Real close.

As they arced across the first causeway leading to Miami Beach, magnificent stretches of blue water dominated the landscape, prompting the audience sitting in the rear bench seat to explode with jubilant cries of "The beach!!! The beach!!!" The unveiling of the Atlantic Ocean spurred the trio to excitedly point in every direction toward the aqua-blue waters surrounding Miami Beach as if they had just sighted land after wandering lost in the ocean for weeks, sailing on inner tube rafts to escape Cuba. The imagined scent of coconut suntan lotion permeated their senses, but there still remained one more causeway to cross before the car dutifully wheeled into its final destination.

A cocktail of a salty breeze and humidity greeted them at the Bancroft Hotel. Located at 15th Street and Collins Avenue, this property on the beach provided spacious rooms with kitchenettes, an Olympic-size outdoor pool, a hole-in-the-wall hamburger shack by the pool, and a thoroughfare to the beach. Most importantly, the Bancroft was situated within walking distance of other Art Deco–inspired hotels favored by northern metro Cuban tribes for their summer vacation, such as the Surfcomber, DiLido, Shorecrest, St. Moritz, and Delano.

Like a swarm of locusts, for the next two to three weeks, Cuban clans would congregate to immerse themselves in sun, pool, and ocean, and would delight in the early-morning sultry smells of guava pastries or freshly baked Cuban bread, because fathers like Esteban's drove every day to Little Havana to retrieve authentic Cuban pastries for breakfast.

On the third day of their vacation, Esteban mustered up the courage to put his imagined *Sea Hunt* skills to the test and venture into the surf with his speargun. He snorkeled out to some rocks with a friend, where they saw decent-sized fish darting around. He loaded the speargun, pulled the trigger, and watched the death throes of an innocent fish. Mercilessly tearing the fish off the spear as if he were a sea nomad from the Bajau tribe in Indonesia, Esteban triumphantly waded back to shore and boasted to his father, after scarfing down a guava pastry, that he had passed the first test in becoming a sea explorer like Lloyd Bridges. He spent the rest of the day reliving his underwater exploration in slow motion. That night, Esteban could hardly sleep in anticipation of the morning's underwater exploits.

As soon as rays of light snuck through the window blinds the following morning, Esteban arose, quietly gathered his equipment, and stealthily snuck out of the room. There were several seagulls gliding around, small crabs scurrying to their tiny holes in the sand, and some pelicans floating on the water, but Esteban was the only human being on the beach. The excursion of the day before boosted his confidence about this morning's adventure.

As he looked out toward the horizon, he daydreamed that he would spear a fish big enough to feed everyone at dinner. The ocean was calm and the water clear. Low tide revealed a huge, flat rock about seventy-five feet from shore. Esteban decided it would be a perfect location to launch his adventure. He waded out to the rock and discovered that he, who stood just shy of six feet tall, was in about five feet of water. He proceeded to throw all of his gear onto the sun-heated rock, clambered up, and paused to look over the serene green-blue waterscape, content with his mastery. After basking in the sun for a couple of minutes, he put on his fins, secured the snorkel to his face mask, and pulled back the elastic band of the speargun to load it. With a nod to his mentor, he shouted through the snorkel, "Let's go, Lloyd," and slipped down the rock and into the warm depths.

As his fins hit the ocean floor, he felt some turbulence around him, and it was then that he noticed two large, shadowy marine creatures swim past him. They were large, as long as Esteban was tall, and thick in girth. He couldn't discern if they were sharks, dolphins, or some other form of aquatic alien invader. He looked warily at the size of his spear and compared it to the size of the denizen of the deep, quickly deducing that his weapon would have the effect of a toothpick piercing a Tomahawk-bone steak and would just serve to piss off these potentially dangerous aquatic life-forms.

Esteban immediately opted for the safety of the rock, and there he sat and scoured the ocean for ten minutes, waiting for his composure to return. He hoped the predators had moved on. The whole episode had lasted only a couple of minutes, and the beach remained deserted. He imagined Lloyd Bridge's voice calling an end to the day's adventure, and resigned himself that his seafaring life as a *Sea Hunt* protégé had ended as quickly as it had started.

He anxiously calculated the distance he had to cover to safely reach the shore. After a couple of meditative minutes silently praying for clear waters that were devoid of threatening marine life, Esteban leapt into the water, furiously flailing with every one of his appendages until he crawled out of the ocean and found his way back to his hotel. He snuck quietly back into his room, making sure not to wake his parents, rolled under the bedcovers, and waited for the scent of guava pastries to pierce the air.

Although this celebrated summer sojourn to Miami Beach had been embraced by many Cuban-American families as one of their newly created customs in the United States, it was not the only significant one they would develop. After the Cuban reunion (of sorts) in Miami Beach had elapsed into a sentimental summer memory, the period between Thanksgiving and Christmas became a meaningful time for Cubans recently arrived in New York to both preserve their island's traditions and partake in a custom that would unequivocally affirm their zeal for becoming part of the iconic Norman Rockwell American landscape they had dreamt of.

Cuba was the only island in the Caribbean to have benefited from the great experiment of American radio and television media technology. It was the first Latin American country where television was test-marketed in 1946, and in 1958 it was the second country in the world with access to color television. In addition, Cuba boasted the largest radio audience in the Caribbean (which was adroitly utilized to promote and galvanize the Cuban Revolution). Prior to the 1958 revolution, the technological reach of Western media exposed millions of Cubans to American values, which were interpreted as either a wonderful testament to freedom or a morally corrupt example of capitalism.

However, there was one iconic American institution that was immune to criticism and universally regarded as a mecca of wholesome entertainment. It consisted of Hollywood movies projected onto the largest screen in America and an augmented show featuring a renowned troupe of dancers—the famous Rockettes. The legendary entertainment venue, fondly nicknamed the Showplace of the Nation, was Radio City Music Hall.

When the greens of Central Park foliage changed to reds, oranges, and yellows, Cubans made a pilgrimage to Radio City Music Hall to celebrate the winter holidays and take another symbolic step in their immersion into American culture. Along with reciting the Pledge of Allegiance, this seasonal pilgrimage was a primary Cuban rite of passage, in which they would be proudly welcomed as new members of their adopted American homeland.

The never-ending wait for that special day would come to a wonderfully tantalizing conclusion on the Sunday after Thanksgiving. The itinerary was always meticulously planned in the following order: morning Mass, bus into the city, and an early lunch at a Chinese restaurant. Then it would be time for the big show. The older Cuban adults saw participating in the annual family ritual not only as a celebration of the pomp and circumstance surrounding attendance at a Radio City Music Hall performance (similar to that of the traditional Easter Parade and Bonnet Festival, where revelers gather around St. Patrick's Cathedral and stroll up and down 5th Avenue showcasing their new headwear), but also as an opportunity to distinguish themselves from other immigrants and squelch the perception of Cuba as a banana republic. It was a public-relations affirmation that Cubans are honorable and undeniably contributing members of American society.

Consequently, before the family left their apartment to embark on their fanciful annual excursion, Rolando and Onaydis momentarily subdued the untamed excitement exhibited by the children by insisting on paternal order and social decorum. Just as the Radio City Rockettes donned their wardrobe for their matinee performance, Cuban families meticulously prepared for their appearance at the iconic American venue by dressing in a way that reflected their pride, self-respect, and commitment to enhancing their cultural and social status. The working theme for the day was to "dress to fit in, and hopefully impress," and the kids were, naturally, the first to be dressed.

Esteban and Eduardo squirmed uncomfortably in an attempt to relieve the incessantly itchy matching wool jackets and shorts in a traditional gray houndstooth pattern. Their outfits were completed with pairs of equally matching, and perfectly polished, black Thom McAn dress shoes (a quintessential American brand established in 1922), long white socks reaching to just below their kneecaps, a white shirt whose collar was one size too small, and a black-tie finish. In effect, the boys' apparel seemed to have been inherited from Little Lord Fauntleroy's fictional British estate. In contrast, Maria was sporting an impishly adorable ballet-style outfit, and her curly hair was styled to mimic one of America's original sweethearts, Shirley Temple. As a final elegant touch, Onaydis accentuated her daughter's fashionable ensemble by enclosing her in an aristocratic English riding coat. The three kids looked like they were part of the cast for the classic cinematic family gem *Mary Poppins*, which was, in fact, the movie feature they were on their way to see.

Onaydis proudly proclaimed her children ready for public view as she tied their ties, brushed their hair, and sat them in place, warning of severe consequences if they were to engage in any activity that directly or indirectly creased any part of their finely pressed outfits or, God forbid, mussed their hair.

Both parents prepared for their appearance by emulating movie stars from their respective period of film fascination, with Rolando donning a perfectly appointed suit that was inspired by the "definition of debonair" actor Cary Grant, while Onaydis complemented her husband's sophisticated swagger and highlighted her graceful demeanor with a sophisticated ensemble reminiscent of Elizabeth Taylor (minus the multi-diamond hardware).

The weather that day was slightly brisk and sunny, which offered the two grateful boys a slight reprieve from their wool-infused itchy-skin angst, and set the stage for an incredibly magical setting in which to embrace the exquisite charms of New York City.

After the show, the three kids were exhilarated and happy, as if they had just had all their wishes granted, and Onaydis and Rolando silently gazed at each other, relishing their own happiness. They also poignantly acknowledged that their attempt to transition their generational Cuban traditions to an American cultural custom such as attending the winter holiday shows at Radio City Music Hall had been successful, and had resulted in an extraordinary family day. As both parents realized that this experience was one well worth repeating on an annual basis, Onaydis tugged on Rolando's elbow, and lovingly whispered, "Rolando, this is now our new life. What could be more American than this?"

"And Cuban as well, Onaydis."

Chapter 8

In which early weekend hours at the shop find Esteban entertaining ladies of the night and Vinny is saved by Maria, but with wiseguy consequences.

It was early Sunday morning and Esteban and the crew were preparing for the usual onslaught of customers, including the regulars who were wise to coming early, before the rush took hold, to enjoy the shop's special Sunday breakfast items. Vinny, a larger-than-life character and successful restaurateur who, inexplicably, was not regaled with his own giant helium balloon in Macy's Thanksgiving Day Parade—and a collegial friend of the three Cubans—had secured a table in the farthest corner of the bagel shop to ensure privacy for him and his drop-dead gorgeous "friend."

Vinny was a peripheral and otherwise pretend mob guy whose closest connection to the Family was a far-distant third cousin who was a genuine wiseguy and the three Italian eateries he owned. His restaurants were very popular because they always served fresh home-style Italian dishes. And Vinny was very hands-on, presenting himself as an honorary caricature of an Italian eatery's "made man." One restaurant had a Frank Sinatra vibe (Frank Sinatra and the Rat Pack were on constant audible rotation), another was adorned with *Sopranos* memorabilia, and the third was resplendent with tchotchkes from famous mob movies, including *Goodfellas*, *Casino*, and *The Godfather*.

Miguel, Maria, and Esteban frequently ate at his restaurants, where they would watch with admiration as Vinny engaged his patrons as if he were the ringmaster of a circus—or, in his mind, the Godfather of his domain. And the domain decorated with kitschy gangland mementos unintentionally and rather unfortunately attracted real-life mob fellas. But, as Vinny had once explained to Esteban, he was not inclined to become a true-to-life made man or attract this constituency to his tables. He did not want mob guys coming to his restaurant for a couple of reasons, the first being the likelihood of an unsuspecting diner ending up face down in his pasta e fagioli courtesy of a .38, and the second that certain wiseguy diners told the waitstaff to put their check on their tab, which of course would never make its way to accounts receivable.

Vinny was understandably nervous that something bad would occur, especially to him. Esteban, who could read the depth of Vinny's anxiety, thought for a moment and then proposed a brilliantly simple solution.

"Vinny—let it be known that your insurance company is requesting that you put cameras in your restaurants. But here's the trick. You don't actually purchase any cameras. You just start a rumor by talking to some regulars within earshot of other folks.

You act irritated about more expenses you have to suck up to keep your insurance premiums down. That should take care of it, because none of those guys are gonna want to be seen in your home movies, especially if they're not with their wife."

It worked like magic. Somewhat immediately, a couple of the wiseguys stopped showing up, and soon all of them stopped altogether. Vinny never purchased any cameras and never collected on the debts he was owed, but he didn't care as he was now back in control of his businesses and safely back in his pretend wiseguy world.

On Sunday mornings at seven, like clockwork, Vinny would show up at the bagel shop with his gumad and order a gaggle of breakfast items, including bagel sandwiches, empanadas, and flans, to replenish carbs expended during their sexual gymnastics the night before. The lovebirds cooed as they fed each other by hand, and then, much to the amusement of the shop's staff, in an effort to maintain a modicum of discretion would depart before the Sunday rush arrived. Vinny would drive his gumad home in his inconspicuous tangerine Maserati.

About half an hour later, he would return to gloat to Esteban about his previous night's activities and order takeout for his own family's Sunday breakfast. All the employees knew of Vinny's philandering exploits, and their impression of him was divided by gender. The women thought him despicable, while the fellas admired his harem and his car. Vinny's lifestyle was celebrated by most but rebuked by some.

By eight a.m. the bagel shop was a kaleidoscope of characters populating a flour-and-empanada-scented circus. Like Vinny and his gumad, other Saturday night partiers would bumble into the shop for something to eat—and they were not searching for healthy fare like egg whites and oatmeal to offset their hangover from the previous night's escapades. They were craving a much-needed dose of eggs, cheese, and grease and more grease in the form of bacon, sausage, ham, or pork roll.

Esteban loved these customers for several reasons. The most important, in Esteban's mind, was that they always paid in cash, albeit sometimes smelly cash. Many of the early-bird customers were women coming off their night's work, which consisted of two shifts. Four and sometimes five of them would show up for breakfast after having danced at a gentleman's club a few blocks away, and for their second shift would entertain their best clients in a hotel directly across the street from the bagel shop.

The bills often carried a range of pervasive scents, which Esteban would later present to Maria as examples of exotic perfumes that he would ask her to identify, and half-jokingly suggest that she consider purchasing one of the scents. And that led to the second reason why Esteban was particularly enamored with these customers—the comic relief they generated. These were loyal customers who, despite the long nights, engaged in witty, comical, and slightly affectionate and flirtatious banter. They relished the opportunity to play with Esteban as if he were a naive young kid drooling to get laid.

"Good morning, ladies, I trust everyone slept well. When I see you goddesses, it's like I'm watching the sun rise, and I know I'm gonna have a good day!"

The accepted matriarch of the lady's group, Alicia, a distinguished-looking Black woman with seductive legs that were much longer than her upper torso, leaned over the counter and whispered, "It was good, but it woulda been great if you were there, honey," as she moistened her lips with her tongue.

Then Brianna would step forward. "Esteban, you a good-looking, strong Latino man and you don't know what you are capable of unless you wid women like us."

And another woman joined the chorus, shouting, "Like cha-cha-and-cha, baby!"

Clearly shaken and stirred, Esteban blushed, but quickly recovered. "You ladies don't know what you're missing," he said as he did an awkward imitation of a Michael Jackson moon dance away from the counter so that his hard-on wouldn't butt heads with the cash register.

The male employees observing this verbal jousting wished they were standing in Esteban's place. When they saw the convoy of women headed toward the store, they jostled for position, as if boxing out in the paint for a rebound, trying to get to the front of the store and behind the counter. However, Esteban would put a halt to their forward progress with a simple gesture and a stern look.

As the women collected their orders, Esteban was the recipient of a bundle of tightly rolled perfumed bills. Some of the males wanted a sniff, but Pepe outsmarted them by asking Esteban for change for a hundred-dollar bill.

Mo brought Vinny's order to the counter, and Esteban yelled out "Vinny!" and waved at him. Vinny was pacing back and forth on the sidewalk, having an animated conversation on his phone. Esteban wondered briefly what the call was about, but dropped the thought. There were things to do.

Moments later, Vinny burst through the door and went up to Esteban. "I need a pound of lox, a pound of whitefish, a pound of the cran-tuna, ten chipotle chicken empanadas, and a dozen bagels—four onion, four everything, two cinnamon raisin, and two garlic bagels!"

"You get one more, Vinny. It's a baker's dozen."

"OK. Give me three garlics, then."

Vinny was uncharacteristically distressed, and Esteban thought it peculiar that the order he had originally placed with the shop, to take home only a couple of sandwiches, was now substantially increased. Vinny asked that the bagels be given to him first.

"Why don't you wait for your whole order?" asked Esteban.

"Because I need the bagels to smell up my car so I smell like them when I get out."

"What?" Esteban was confused.

Vinny got closer to Esteban. "Smell me."

"What? Get the fuck outta here." Esteban pushed Vinny away, not wanting any part of smelling Vinny like a dog at a fire hydrant.

"Seriously, smell me and tell me if you smell a woman's perfume. C'mon, dude. Seriously."

Esteban cautiously leaned in, thinking it was some kind of perverted joke, and proclaimed, "Holy shit, Vinny! You do smell like 'Eau de I've been fucking around.' You reek of adultery cologne, dude! But what do you care? Didn't you tell me your wife was with her parents this weekend?"

"That's what I thought until I just got this call saying her and her parents are driving down to have breakfast with everyone! Her parents want to take the kids to the zoo!"

Esteban handed Vinny the thirteen onion, garlic, cinnamon raisin, and everything bagels. "Here you go. The rest of your order is coming up."

Vinny grabbed the bagels. "I'm putting these in my car and closing the windows, and by the time I get in with the rest of the order, my car will smell like this bagel shop."

"Vinny. You actually think that 'Eau de everything, onion, cinnamon raisin, and garlic bagels' will cover up that perfume?" asked Esteban as he grimaced. "That's not going to cover up that smell. It's just gonna smell like bagels baked by Dior. Don't you think Donna is gonna ask you if we're now making a Chanel-scented fucking bagel?"

At that moment, Maria cheerfully walked through the front door. Esteban abruptly stopped talking and Vinny turned to Maria as she greeted them.

"Hola, guys! How are you doing, Vinny? Miguel and me went to your place for dinner last night, and it was great! As always!"

Maria had arrived later than usual. On Sundays, she would usually show up to the store around seven to make sure the food items were fresh and ready for the morning rush. She skidded to a stop, lifted her nose toward the sky, and turned around to face Esteban and Vinny. Vinny pulled out a pair of sunglasses and poked himself in the eye with the tip as he frantically tried to put them on, thinking the shades made him invisible. "Did the girls come and go already?" she asked, referring to the trace aroma left by their scented bills.

"Ah, yeah. They just left," said Esteban. "Why? You can smell their money?" Maria possessed a sense of smell that was supernatural for a human being. "How the fuck can you smell that? Are you part bear?"

Maria mockingly attributed her magical gift of scent to a blood transfusion she had received at an animal hospital, one that came from a bloodhound.

"No, this is different. Which one of you has Chanel N°5 on?"

Maria slowly approached Esteban and sniffed, and then turned her attention to Vinny. Her nostrils contracted, causing her to squint her eyes, and with hands on hips she suspiciously asked, "Vinny—why weren't you at the restaurant last night? We thought it was strange that you weren't there on a Saturday night."

Vinny stood stoically, doing his best to imitate a zombie, clutching the bag of bagels. Then his lips moved. "How could you possibly know that's Chanel N°5?"

"Because I buy that perfume for my mom, Vinny. Now stop it and straighten up. Esteban, do you know about this?"

"About what?"

"Did Donna go visit her mom? Is Donna home, Vinny?" asked Maria. She assumed he was picking breakfast up for the family.

"Yeah."

"Yeah what?" Maria continued her interrogation.

"Yeah, she went to visit her mother, and yeah, she's coming back home this morning. And she's coming back with her parents to have breakfast with the kids AND GO TO THE ZOOOO!"

Maria's motherly instincts kicked in. "Vinny! Buckle up, Vinny! Does your car smell like this?"

"Yeah."

"Go put your bag of bagels in the car and come back. Leave the bag open. Hurry up."

Vinny ran the bagels to his car, which he always illegally parked right outside the front door of the shop. He came back like a shot to stand in front of the court of Maria and beg for mercy.

"Esteban, trade shirts with Vinny."

"I can't switch shirts with him!"

Vinny interjected, "I'm a double XL."

"And I'm a large! You need a guy twice my size."

"Hector!" Maria yelled. "Come over here, please."

Hector was a grill cook and also happened to be the largest person in the store. His stomach protruded so far out that his belly was always bumping into the front of the grill. Fortunately, Hector had been born with arms long enough to not only scratch his knees but, more importantly, reach the grill to cook. Vinny was his physiological equivalent.

"Hector, how would you like a beautiful green Lacoste golf shirt?" Maria asked. The color of his shirt, in Vinny's estimation, was the perfect complement to his Maserati's shade of tangerine.

"No me gusta ese color, jefa."

Maria said to Hector, "Bueno. El necesita cambiar su camisa con la tuya. Yo te compro otra camisa nueva. La camisa que quieras." Then, turning to Vinny, she explained she would buy Hector any shirt he wanted, but Vinny would still have to part with his.

Hector shrugged his shoulders. "Bueno. Lo que usted desea, jefa."

She pointed to the back of the store and instructed Vinny and Hector to exchange garments in the refrigerator room.

"No need to worry, Vinny. You're like a brother to us, and we protect our family. Leave the rest of your order here."

Within five minutes, Hector was back at the grill, happily sporting a green Lacoste golf shirt, while Vinny was wearing a t-shirt that had multiple grease stains and smelled like empanadas and bacon instead of Chanel N°5.

While picking off dry tuna salad from the chest area, Vinny opined, "This shirt sucks."

"As opposed to the alternative?" Maria chuckled. "It smells better than Chanel N°5, right?"

"Never mind." Vinny stuffed a twenty-dollar bill in the tip jar, shouting, "Molte grazie, Hector!"

From the grill came "Gracias a usted, Mr. Vinny!"

Maria handed Vinny the last of his order and, with a final sniff, declared him to be perfume-free. She capitalized on the opportunity to lovingly blackmail him. "Vinny, no worries, papi. That's two pounds of lox and twenty empanadas every Sunday—right?"

"Yes, Maria. Every Sunday."

"And happy hour at your restaurant, every day, anytime, right?"

"Esteban? Are you gonna let your sister roll me like this?"

"I grew up with her, Vinny. She was part of the Cuban mafia. But it's a small price to pay for protection. You know about protection, dude."

"Let me get out of here before I have to give away my restaurants."

"Love you, Vinny. Say hi to Donna for us." Maria turned to her brother. "I wonder what story Vinny will invent about Hector's shirt."

CHAPTER 9

In which a friend from the Dominican Republic shares stories from the streets of LA and to whom Miguel reveals the secret of how to "Americanize" a Spanish accent.

Paradise, Miguel thought as he deftly boogied through the back of the bagel shop, inhaling the energy and noting the looks of surprise as he crisscrossed through the hustle-and-bustle traffic jam of customers and employees until he reached his destination, his treasured relic, his Ark of the Covenant—the grill. It was noon on a Wednesday, and Miguel had decided to forgo his usual lunchtime routine at his office in favor of creating a unique lunchtime treat for himself. He hadn't decided on what the treat would be, figuring the shop would speak to him.

After scanning the shop's delicacies, Miguel narrowed down his choices, repeating to himself, "This is truly a paradise." There were two finalists worthy of consideration. "Should I put together a breakfast special that includes three eggs over-easy with crackling crispy corned beef hash and charred hash browns prepared with freshly diced onions and jalapeños, doused in ketchup and hot sauce? Or do I prepare a rye, spicy mustard, and three-inch-thick Tower of Power pastrami sandwich, my version of the famous Katz Deli pastrami experience?"

Miguel chose to replicate the Katz Deli pastrami experience.

He had never been a cook, much less a chef, but he loved food—every kind of food—and he was one of the fortunate few not to have any food allergies. He was free to indulge in gastronomic delights from any culture, which, in turn, was one of his compelling motivations to delve into the adventures of cooking. He had known his way around a kitchen from an early age because his mother hated to waste her time in the kitchen and would put the least amount of effort possible into making food palatable, never mind inviting.

For Miguel, the bagel shop represented a culinary holiday where he could express any tradition festively in the form of food and spices. It was theater that delivered another level of interaction with the customers and allowed Miguel to take full creative liberties with all of the kitchen tools and food items at his disposal.

He hung up his suit jacket beside the bagel-rolling table, strapped on an apron, rolled up his sleeves, and cozied up to the prep station to assemble his ingredients, salivating from the beguiling aroma of fat rising up from the hot, greasy grill—an aroma that would permeate his pores and linger on his finely tailored corporate outfit as if he were a walking exhaust pipe.

Esteban strolled up to the prep station. "What are you making for lunch today, dude?"

"I'm going full nuclear Katz Deli because I'm hungry, and getting hungrier the more I think about it."

Esteban had been watching Miguel's pre-grill warm-up routine, and knew exactly what he meant, because he was a Katz Deli aficionado as well and knew about their behemoth pastrami sandwiches. "When my sister comes by, I'll let her know you won't be having any dinner tonight, Miguel."

Miguel finished preparing the sandwich and was looking forward to closing his office door to enjoy the obscenely colossal pastrami tower. Based on its square footage, he estimated that his taste buds would be wonderfully entertained for about thirty minutes, and God help the person who interrupted this delight—unless it was his boss. He flung his apron into the dirty linen basket, wrapped up his gastronomical rendition of bliss (it was so heavy it could have served as an anchor on a cruise ship), and was on his way out of the kitchen when he noticed a favorite customer at the front of the shop who, over time and after many revealing, confidential bartender-style conversations, had become a friend.

The Dominican man, like many of their other Hispanic customers, had made a Latino connection—spiritual and culinary—with the three Cubans and the shop. They spent social time at the shop as if they were hanging out in their neighborhood bar, barbershop, or bodega. Miguel, Maria, and Esteban were cultural descendants of a Caribbean island (and Spain too, because many Latin American nations were inhabited by the Spanish during their commissioned voyages of exploration), and the shop featured a range of special Spanish and Cuban "grandma recipes" that appealed to the predominantly Caribbean Hispanics from the 'hood.

"Yo, Papo! What's up, my man?" Miguel greeted his friend. Papo was wearing a suit whose pants looked like they'd been fashioned from a hotel bedcover made of highly flammable polyester, with a stylish top layer presumably woven out of fiberglass. Miguel waved at his friend to join him in a quiet corner of the shop.

"Nothing much, Miguel. Same old, same old. Damn, you looking good! You clean up nice!"

"Yeah. Just stoppin' by from my weekday job to get some food."

"What the fuck, bro? Is that a Brooks Brothers suit?"

Papo was a street hustler who owned a back-alley clothing and accessory store that featured top-brand designer fashion lines at enticing but conspicuously suspect pricing. It was strictly a cash business, and he acquired all of his merchandise from "special friends and associates" who worked in the garment district in New York City and provided Papo with merchandise that was inexplicably rerouted from its original, legitimate commercial destination into his domain. He had established a fervent following of well-to-do society patrons, men and women, who would frequent his store hoping for an opportunity to bump into designer clothing, shoes, jewelry, and so on in their sizes, and at fifty percent less than what they would pay at a retail store. And his "special friends and associates" loved him as well because he had ingeniously crafted a highly credible reputation as a trustworthy purveyor of authentic merchandise who was never delinquent on paying for the goods he purchased.

"Do you want to buy some designer sunglasses, Miguel? Some nice shades landed on my lap."

"Nah, Papo. I'm good with shades. But if you land

any black Ferragamo rides, I'd be interested."

Papo displayed a brief expression of disappointment, but like any good salesman, quickly disregarded the momentary setback, and offered Miguel another opportunity. "How about all your white friends? Can you get any of them to come my way and check out my shop? I'll take care of you, my man."

"Yeah, I can do that, no problem, but I expect a vig. Fifteen percent."

"Fifteen percent? Are you fucking crazy, man?"

Miguel took the opportunity to demonstrate to his friend why he was the better salesman. "That's eighty-five percent more than you would have had without me."

There was a momentary silence between the two as Papo weighed the cost of doing business with Miguel. "OK. You got it."

"I'll bring them by personally. No disrespect, but my friends are not used to buying shit that falls off of a truck. Once they see they can bring back legit shit for half the price, they'll be customers for life. But don't discount it to half price right off the bat."

Papo was amused by Miguel's suggestion. "Yeah, yeah, I got you. We'll start at thirty percent off, then go to forty percent because they're *your* friends. I can't go to a fifty percent discount because I have to pay your vig."

They smiled in agreement.

This was the first time Miguel had seen Papo in the last couple of weeks, and he was curious where he had been. "Didn't you say you were going out west to LA?"

"Yup. Just got back yesterday."

"What'd you say you were doing out there? Going out for a concert? How'd it go?"

"Great concert. My buddy was the producer. He put together a bunch of salsa and merengue acts from the Dominican Republic and Puerto Rico."

"Wow. But wait. What about mariachis? Weren't there any mariachis?"

"No. No fucking mariachis, even though, ironically enough, my producer friend is actually Mexican. And he also had a fucking great DJ. Place was rocking. Sold out."

"Any Puerto Rican and Dominican people show up? Or how 'bout Cubans? Any Cubans go?"

"There had to be Cubans there, Miguel. I mean, it was mostly Puerto Ricans and Dominicans, and a couple of Mexicans thrown into the salsa as well. There were like ten thousand people there. It was like I was hanging out in Washington Heights, except I wasn't stepping on any fuckin' crack vials."

"Yeah. Not too many Cubans out in LA. Not like here or Miami, anyway. So, this was the first time in LA for you? How long were you there?" asked Miguel.

"Yeah, Miguel. Believe it or not, it was the first time. Just four days. But we got around. Went to Santa Monica—"

"Did you go to the pier?"

"Yeah, went to the pier, nice place. And checked out Venice Beach as well."

Miguel shrugged, rolled his eyes, and smirked in a demonstration of cynicism. "Venice Beach is a unique place. It's not my flavor."

"I know what you mean, Miguel. It's fucking interesting, though, entertaining, with all the characters there. But they are some crazy fuckers there. I mean, forget about free spirits. More like lost souls. And a shit ton of homeless. Everywhere. Even in Santa Monica. Like they take up every square inch of ground, bro."

"It's like that throughout the state, Papo. The homeless are everywhere. It's like a destructive social experiment. Like social anarchy. I used to go out there a bunch of times for business, and would bounce around all over the place. It was on the company dime, so why wouldn't I? Beautiful place, great weather, but you never know what you're going to run into. Too many people in a state of mental decay, with no real access to help, or people who are criminals with nothing to lose out there. It's like a lawless land."

"You're right, dude. Too many. I feel safer in Washington Heights. But I gotta tell you, even though we were only there for four days, we had some funny shit happen."

Miguel smiled, anticipating a strange tale. "Like what?"

"So we're riding around, driving to these places with my producer friend, when he decides to stop at some big-box store in east LA to pick up some print paper and Sharpies. I'm standing around with my friend while the producer disappears to get his shit, when all of a sudden, over the loudspeaker, I hear 'Damas y caballeros, this is US Immigration and Customs Enforcement. Please proceed to the front of the store so we can check your immigration status.'"

"Whaaat?" Miguel reacted in shock. "What the fuck happened? Did ICE conduct a raid? In LA? Thank God *you* weren't fucking deported back to the DR, Papo!"

As they broke out into laughter, Papo shot back with, "Fuck you, Miguel. Just 'cause you're a fucking white boy that was born here. But, bro, listen, the whole fuckin' store clears out. Everybody ran the fuck out. The whole store. It looked like a scene out of a zombie apocalypse. Carts were left all over the store, all full of shit. There were carts all through the store, but no one around. Even a lot of employees bolted. Me and my friend are freaking out. We don't know what to do. I have never seen anything like this. And then my producer friend comes back, and he's laughing his ass off."

Confusion was written all over Miguel's face.

"And he tells us that it was his voice on the overhead! He says, 'Papo, I couldn't help it. I just saw the microphone lying there with nobody around, and I had to do something, and when I looked around the store and saw all the illegals, I thought it would be funny. Nobody stopped me.'"

"Wait, dude. Didn't you say your producer friend is Mexican?"

"Yeah, dude. Fuckin' Mexican. He don't give a shit. That's why he thought it was funny. And when we walk outside, no one is around. No one. Like fuckin' nothing but—what do you call those balls of grass or twigs or whatever gettin' blown around in the open, all dusty and shit, like in old Western movies?"

"You mean tumbleweeds?"

"Yeah, that's it. Tumbleweeds. It's like he conducted a fuckin' social experiment with his own people in a fuckin' store."

"That's crazy, Papo. It is funny, though."

"Yeah, well, the fucked-up shit, Miguel, was that it was obvious that everyone in the store was illegal. That's just one store, bro! I mean, there must be neighborhoods out there with nothing but illegals. It's goddamn crazy!"

"Glad you got to see that shit, Papo. California is chock-full of illegals from everywhere, and homeless. We can give the illegals welfare, education, health care, and driver's licenses, but we can't take care of our homeless. That's crazy town right there."

"Without a doubt, it is crazy town. But check this

out, because that was nothing compared to what happened that night with my friend. You never know what's going to happen with this guy."

"Oh, I can't wait to hear this." Miguel's lingering hunger had given way to curiosity about Papo's comical misadventures. "OK, so nighttime comes, and what?"

"We're staying at the same downtown Hyatt as the producer. So, because he booked a bunch of rooms, like a whole floor, for him and his crew, the manager of the hotel invites him to dinner and says to bring a couple of the crew. So the producer asks me and one of my friends if we want to come with him to dinner. We join the producer and the manager for an exclusive dinner in a private suite, and then the room starts to shake."

"No shit, Papo! You were in an earthquake? I would have shit in my pants."

"Actually, it wasn't that bad. It was over in like twenty seconds. Then, after everything stops shaking, the manager says, 'Hey, do you guys want to go for a ride into Hollywood?' and we all agree to go. I offer to drive the car I rented."

"You went cruising? Seriously? Where'd you guys go?"

"We pile into the car. I'm driving. The manager is riding shotgun and my friend and the producer are riding in the back. This manager looks like he fell out of a fuckin' preppy-of-the-year calendar. I mean, he's wearing this cute little cardigan with a sports jacket, penny loafers, and a perfect fucking hairdo. He looks like he came straight out of Yale."

"Sounds like a Ralph Lauren WASP from New England."

"That's exactly it, Miguel. So he says, 'Let's drive

down Sunset Boulevard and look for some whores.' But we just want to sightsee, not bring them back with us."

"Whores? You went looking for whores?"

"No, no. We just want to see the action, not be a part of it. So we drive down Sunset, and nothing. It's empty. No one on the streets and nothing to see. Then the manager suggests, 'Let's drive down Melrose. Maybe there's something going on there.' Off we go to Melrose Avenue. As I turn onto Melrose, we see packs of four or five women strolling. Maybe they had all moved from Sunset to Melrose?"

"That's strange. Every time I went to LA, all the activity was on Sunset. Melrose was like the B or C team."

"Well, there was nothing happening on Sunset, so we're all goofing around, talking shit, until the producer yells from the back seat, '¡Ay chingao! They're men! They're not women! These women are men!'"

Miguel's eyes opened wide as he looked at Papo. "What? What are you talking about?"

"Miguel, they were men."

"What the fuck? Are you serious? How could you tell from the car that they were men?"

"Dude, there were a lotta streetlights, and it became pretty obvious that the producer was right. It became clear as day, even from the car at night! The producer says, 'Look at their fucking hands! Look at their knees! Check out their Adam's apples! These putas are maricón putos.'

"After he says that, we all start to take a closer look, and then we see hands and knees that are skanky-ass big. I mean, now we see mitts for hands and knees so huge they look like they belong to a pro lineman, and believe me, they were having a tough time walking in their heels. No question they are men. We are in fuckin' shock noticing this, *and* feel even more fucked-up at not having noticed it from the start. And you're not gonna believe what happens next." Papo paused for effect. "There's a group of women on the corner, except they're hangin' out by the drive-through lanes of a bank. The bank is closed for the night, and there aren't any lights on, and there's like five or six of them in the shadows, so you actually can't really tell …"

"OK, c'mon," urged Miguel.

"So, Miguel, the hotel manager, thinking he was cute—"

"Oh no."

"He lowers his window and, in bad Spanish, starts yellin', '¡Oye, mami! ¡Oye, chiquitas!' while he puckers up and squeals out kisses at them."

Miguel began to suspect an unforced error was about to befall the instigator.

"Bro, there's a lot of traffic, so we're moving slow, and some of the girls start moving toward the car. Then we gotta stop for a red light. We're at a dead stop, and this guy continues throwing kisses and keeps yelling out 'chiquitas' and shit. And as they come out of the shadows, one of these chicks yells back, 'Oh look, ladies! Is Mr. Hyatt! Mr. Hyatt, hello, my lovely.' Then the other women join in the chorus, and they all began blowing him kisses and yelling, 'Mr. Hyatt! Oh, you looking good, baby! Looking good, Mr. Hyatt!' Bro, when the group got closer, it was obvious that these were men that were dressed like women."

"Holy shit, Papo."

"They were transvestites, bro, and friends of the manager. He rolls up his window, looks straight ahead, and ignores these chicks. When the light turns green, he yells, 'Hit it! Let's go! Get out, get out of here!' I think he pissed in his pants. So the producer starts yelling, 'Snagged! Snagged! You fuck around with men! You fucking play with cocks!'"

"Holeee shit. What did this guy do, dude?"

"Nothing. He just sat there, looking straight ahead and not saying shit except that he wanted to go back to the hotel. He never saw what was coming. It was unbelievable. We went back to the hotel and never heard from the fucker again."

"Only in Hollywood."

"Only in Hollywood. That motherfucker is never, ever taking us out to dinner, ever again. But before he ran out of the car, I asked him for ten bucks so I could tip the hotel valet."

"You what?"

"Yeah. I asked him for ten bucks to tip the valet."

"What? You didn't have ten bucks on you?"

"I did after I got the money from him."

Miguel looked at Papo inquisitively.

"He gave me ten and ran out so fast that no one else even had time to get out of the car. So I drove by the valet and self-parked and kept the fucking money!"

"And that taught him a lesson: Don't fuck with people from Joisey! That's some story, Papo. That was fun, thanks. Well, good seeing you. Gotta get back."

"Wait, wait. I gotta ask you a question. Are there a lotta white people at the executive level over there?"

"Yeah. I'm the only Spanish guy out of a hundred. How's that for a diversity ratio? Safe to say, a lot of my friends are white people, but I also have Black friends, like you."

"I'm not Black, Miguel. I'm Dominican."

"Here we go. But you do have black skin? Or do I need cataract surgery?"

"Yes, my skin is black, but I'm Dominican. I'm not Black."

"OK. I'll grant you the Dominican part, but you have to give me the black skin part."

"Fine. You can have the black skin."

"So then, you would be a Black Dominican, right?"

"I would prefer if you refer to me as a Dominican with black skin."

"A black-skinned Dominican."

"Whatever, Miguel. Just make sure you say the word *Dominican* dominantly over *black*."

"You mean, like, whisper *black* followed by a full-throated *Dominican*?"

"That's about right. I'll go with that. Let me ask you another question before you go, to settle my curiosity born out of immigrant ignorance. How does a Cuban guy go through life with a name like Miguel and not have a Spanish accent? 'Cause you don't have a Spanish accent at all. How's that work?"

"Were *you* born here, Papo?"

"No, I got here when I was thirteen. Twenty-three years ago."

"OK. I was born here, but my parents were in the first wave of Cubans that came after Castro's revolution, and you had all these families wanting to make their kids as American as apple pie."

"No más empanadas for you!" said Papo, laughing.

"We still had empanadas, dude, but we had a lot of McDonald's too. In those times, my parents thought that if you wanted to be American, you had to eat McDonald's."

"Didn't you speak Spanish at home?"

"All the time. It was mostly Spanish there, but I spoke English everywhere else. Even my Spanish friends spoke English. Same thing with them."

"So that's where you lost the accent?"

"Nope. All those kids had accents. And the American kids I hung around with also had accents."

"American accents?"

"Yeah, man. Like, you know, regional dialects. Friends from Long Island had a different accent than a friend from Staten Island, even though they're only a couple of miles apart."

"You don't have an accent, or dialect, for that matter."

"Listen, here's the story, then I really gotta run. Three of my cousins lived in a town in Illinois, and they were the only Cubans in town ..."

Miguel had spent the summers of his early youth with first cousins who lived in a moderate-sized suburban village just north of Chicago. The town provided sprawling athletic fields, along with recreational programs that Miguel could enjoy even though he didn't live there. Miguel's parents felt that sending him there was like having him attend summer camp, and it was infinitely better than him spending the summer in the sweltering heat and with the dangerous temptations found on the streets of New York City.

Miguel's cousins represented a rare Cuban outpost in the heartland of America, whose residential demographic landscape was uniformly white. However, they possessed a secret weapon that enabled them to assimilate covertly into the texture of the community: they were all blond and had light complexions, and two had blue eyes (the other had brown eyes). For the Cabrera family—Miguel's aunt, uncle, and cousins—it was a monochromatic vanilla camouflage that made them indistinguishable from the other town residents. Still, they retained one attribute that required modification so as to complete their American cultural conversion: The young Cubans needed to replace their Spanish accent when speaking English with a plain yogurt Midwestern non-accent.

The English language educational curriculum the cousins pursued was not an ESL program or listening to instructional language tapes. Instead, they decided to watch American television—a lot of it. They became fans of black-and-white classic movies like *Casablanca*, *The Maltese Falcon*, *Stagecoach*, *Citizen Kane*, and *Dr. Strangelove*, among others. Every Saturday night at ten p.m., the cousins would congregate around their television, tune in WGN out of Chicago, set themselves up with sodas, chips, deep-dish pizza, popcorn, and chocolate chip cookies, and immerse themselves in the evening's cellulose offerings. The eldest cousin would then give the group a play-by-play of the movie, explaining the plot, describing the professional and personal background of the actors and directors, and pointing out other movies they had acted in or directed. During the week, the three continued to hone their linguistic repertoire by religiously watching *The Johnny Carson Show*. The TV exercise exposed the young Cuban-Americans to American popular culture and social values.

For Miguel, being included in this exercise with his cousins gave him a unique awareness of the American experience. As a bonus, it felt like he had enrolled in a film class.

"I didn't know of and wasn't the slightest bit interested in watching old fucking movies starring Humphrey Bogart, John Wayne, and such shit with my cousins," he told Papo. "At that age, I was making believe I was the Cuban Bruce Lee or Shaft—not fucking Orson Welles."

"Bro, I don't know who the fuck you're talking about. Orson the fuck who? Who names their kid

Orson? What's a fucking Orson? It sounds like a kitchen utensil."

"Shut the fuck up. That's why you'll always be an ign'ant Dominican, like a mangy dog."

"Fuck you and your Cuban superiority, Miguel."

"Stop. Orson Welles was a motherfucker that helped develop the movie industry. Look him up and learn something, dude. Listen—I have to go. So my older cousin was no doubt committed to serving a higher purpose in his version of America, right, and fortunately for me, he forced me to watch and learn from these fuckin' movies. I ultimately came to really appreciate those movies, you know, the art and discipline that goes into making really good movies, and now I am really grateful for his patience and foresight. Then we would stay up late during the week to watch *The Johnny Carson Show*."

"What about Johnny Carson? Who the fuck is Johnny Carson?" asked Papo.

"You hear of Jay Leno? Conan O'Brien? Jimmy Fallon?"

"Yeah, heard of 'em. But I don't watch that late-night shit. I'm doing other things in bed. You know what I mean? I'm not married, bro. I'm a man of action," Papo said as he demonstrated some sexually explicit contortions while attempting to dance an uncoordinated merengue.

"Well, Johnny Carson was before Jay Leno. Jay Leno was before Conan O'Brien, and then came Jimmy Fallon. All these late-night hosts now—Jimmy Fallon, Conan O'Brien, Seth Meyers, Jimmy Kimmel—all these guys owe their career to Johnny Carson. Johnny Carson had the most popular late-night show for decades. He was the King motherfuckin' Kong of all late-night shows. He was a beast."

"So what was the point of your cousin makin' you watch all this shit, Miguel?"

"You ready for this? This is fucked-up. He told me to keep watching Johnny Carson when I got back home, and to try to imitate how he spoke, because Johnny Carson had no distinctive accent, and no one would be able to tell what part or region of the United States you were from, much less Cuba. But the important thing is that whoever you're talking to, even Spanish people, will think you're American. At worst, people will think you're an educated Cuban. And that's how it is, so get used to it, buddy."

Papo looked at Miguel in disbelief.

"Yup. Don't look at me that way, man. That's how it was back then. I know your shit is good, and you're successful, and I am happy for you. But that's what it was like."

"So that's what you did to sound like a white boy? You learned to speak like a white boy from Iowa? If I spoke to you on the phone, I'd think you a white boy."

"My cousin definitely knew what the game was, because even though I may not have had blond hair and blue eyes, I was going to talk like I had blond hair and blue eyes."

"And now you're sellin' bagels in a Jewish deli."

"And Cuban sandwiches and cafés con leche. *And* I'm friends with a Dominican guy that sells hotter stuff than me!"

"You betcha, papi! Welcome to America, Miguel."

"Welcome to our America, Papo."

Chapter 10

In which a conman from North Jersey is treated like a hero when he's released for good behavior and tumbles Esteban to take over the shop to deceive none other than his own mother.

"No matter anyone's ethnicity, their walk of life, political ideology, philosophic bent, or whatever religion they follow, they are made one by the bagel, the most powerful culturally unifying force in the universe. It is so uncomplicated because the bagel shop experience fills the basic human need of allowing oneself to succumb to the devilish pleas from their stomach and heart (in that order) to indulge in an artfully baked delicacy. The blending of high-protein flour, water, salt, yeast, and sugar is a spiritual reward in a morning ritual that celebrates another day of existence."

Esteban had just delivered this sermon to an unsuspecting longtime family acquaintance named Angel, who had stopped by the shop for some breakfast.

"What the fuck, Esteban? What are you, a poet? A philosopher? You've only been at this bagel store for what—a few months?—and you sound like a monk who just came out of a monastery in the Himalayas."

Esteban kept a straight face as he said, "It is a monastery, Angel. A monastery where people come to worship the bagel. It's a religion. It's a fucking way of life, dude."

"You have lost it, my man."

It had been close to a year since Maria, Esteban, and Miguel had bought the store, and while there was still a lot of hard work to do, they were grateful to be witnessing some positive trends. The store seemed to be turning a reputational and financial corner. The employees had leaned into their work, and a healthy team spirit had evolved thanks to, among other things, a bonus system Esteban had instituted on top of salary and tips. The shop was now filled with friendly banter among the customers and staff, who exchanged first names.

Maria was relieved that the goals they had set for the first stage of the shop's transition were largely met, and was cautiously optimistic they were on a growth trajectory. She knew that she, Esteban, and Miguel made a good team and would turn the shop into a welcoming environment with good vibes where people could come for a respite from a complex and hectic world and enjoy the simple pleasures associated with satisfying food.

It was a Saturday morning and the shop was buzzing with activity, orders packaged and sitting on the counter, waiting to be picked up or delivered, and a steady stream of customers waiting to feed their family or their hangovers. The weekend ceremonial activity at the bagel shop was akin to various animal species gathering at the only body of water available at the peak of dry season.

Every weekend without fail, Miguel would punch in for overtime duty from his regular five-day-a-week job to help manage the weekend hordes while Esteban oversaw the cashiers and Maria pushed out baked goods. The frenzy of customers on weekends necessitated an all-hands-on-deck call to action.

As a dedicated fan of movies and popular culture, Miguel helped offset the morning stress by attempting some form of theatrical amusement, performing barely recognizable celebrity impressions while taking food orders from customers. He tried to avoid ethnic or regional accents so he wouldn't appear patronizing or offensive, and impersonated personalities like James Earl Jones, Clint Eastwood, Andrew Dice Clay, Will Ferrell, Marlon Brando as the Godfather, and others. While most customers found the effort amusing, and sometimes joined in with a little improv, others were indifferent and just walked away with ticket in hand, hoping his act would not distract the team from executing their food order.

Emil's booming voice suddenly filled the shop. "Esteban! Buckle up, 'cause Ditto is coming your way!" Emil had exploded through the back door, delivery in hand.

Maria popped out of the freezer. "Did you say you saw Ditto, Emil?"

"Sí, señora. He's coming in now."

Maria stopped what she was doing and moved toward the front of the shop, passing Miguel and muttering, "I can't believe they let Ditto out of jail."

"He's out?" queried Miguel.

"He's not only out, he's here," Maria proclaimed, prompting Miguel to voice something like a howl.

Notable characters had begun to surface at the bagel shop, often as part of their daily ritual. Ditto wasn't the only colorful personality to decorate the shop, as renowned newscasters, singers, Broadway producers, politicians, and rappers started to hang out in a place they saw as a no-longer-so-secret breakfast gem plucked out of the Bowery section of the Lower East Side. They all loved the food and appreciated the polite discretion demonstrated by the customers. And the "average" customers were pleasantly surprised by the cameo appearances and the opportunity to intimately share space with these personalities. Some were treated to an autograph or even a photograph.

The shop was evolving into a popular gathering spot for foodies, famous artists, and Hollywood stargazers, without the paparazzi. The word had gotten out about celebrity sightings there and had effectively transformed the shop into an exciting destination on weekends, with customers hoping to experience the thrill of being around these personalities as they had their "authentic" New York–style bagels and breakfasts.

Ditto may have been all of five feet tall, and weighed about 110 pounds soaking wet. Coming in out of the morning light, he removed his shades and squinted like he was being poked in both eyes. Adjusting to the surroundings, he greeted Esteban. "¿Qué pasa, Esteban?"

Gustavo Perez, aka Ditto, was a Cuban guy who had spent most of his young life engaged with the criminal underworld. As a kid, he attended school according to his own timetable so he could run numbers for some of the Cuban mafia who controlled gambling in a couple of towns in North Jersey. He was nicknamed Ditto at an early age because he had a habit of agreeing with whatever anyone said, and if another person said something that completely contradicted what the first person had said, Ditto would agree with both sides by saying "ditto." He also responded with "ditto" to whatever orders the Cuban mafia guys issued. As he grew older, Ditto proved to be a reliable, productive, and trustworthy member of the local Cuban gang, and was even respected by the other criminal elements in the area.

Ditto's ordained career path, either as a bookie or making license plates in a prison facility, was a destiny made real when the FBI and local law enforcement agencies, acting on years of information provided by informants along with evidence gathered through wiretaps, photos, and protected witnesses, conducted raids and arrested a lot of people, including those doing business in North Jersey. The arrests led to convictions and jail time for key members of the Cuban mafia, and the organized crime faction was functionally dismantled.

Ditto was one of those targeted for arrest, as a ploy to pressure him to provide witness testimony in exchange for his freedom. As it turned out, whether he acted according to the code of honor, whereby one does not rat out one's fellow criminals, or he wanted to avoid the painful repercussions for snitching, Ditto kept his mouth shut and ended up doing a stint in prison. He returned as a respected celebrity because he upheld the code and survived jail time without having been abused or raped; he had been smart enough to pay protection money to powerful entities who ensured his well-being and creature comforts. In fact, when Ditto eventually came out of jail, he looked just as polished as when he went in. Although short and skinny, Ditto was a well-groomed guy who proudly showcased expensive designer clothing and eyewear, and he had the kind of personality people gravitated to.

Upon his early release for good behavior, he

returned to a neighborhood that had been stripped of an organized crime family. Bits and pieces of illegal activity had been absorbed by independent criminal entrepreneurs, but they were of limited intelligence and reluctant to join forces. Ditto had foreseen this and had stashed tens of thousands of dollars in his unsuspecting mother's house prior to going to jail. While incarcerated, he solidified his connections to several sources of ready cash when needed. His foresight allowed him to immediately capitalize on the opportunity to start an underground money-lending enterprise to those whose credit or lifestyle offered no legitimate form of funds. Ditto provided short-term loans for mortgages, new businesses, drug transactions, and gambling—almost anything was on the table for an underground loan—for a nicely profitable return, known in the parlance as a *vig*, in exchange for borrowing his cash. They were all deals that had a short shelf life and a high return.

Miguel and Maria hugged Ditto when he stepped into the shop, while Esteban appraised his attire. "You look good, Ditto. How are things?"

"I'm good. I'm back in business. You need any money?"

"Nah, Ditto, I'm good."

"Not at your rates," said Maria, smirking.

"But if you need some extra capital to lend, then maybe we can talk," Miguel teased Ditto.

Maria cast a cold stare at Miguel and huffed back to the kitchen.

"Well, if any of you know anybody that needs some short-term financial assistance, send 'em my way. I'll cut you in for a finder's fee."

Esteban nonchalantly smiled, ignoring Ditto's proposal.

Then Ditto proffered another request for help. "Esteban, maybe you can help me out with something else. I mean, I would really, really appreciate you helping me on this."

Esteban winced. "What kind of help are you looking for, Ditto?"

"My mom is coming to visit me and some friends, and—"

Esteban interjected, "Your mom? I thought she was still living here with your sister."

"Well, no. Her and my sister moved down to Florida while I was in the tank."

"So what do you need, Ditto?"

"Esteban, she thinks I've gone clean since getting out of jail." Esteban feigned gagging.

"That's good your mom thinks that. Whatever makes her happy, right? With respect, you're not Al Pacino in *Scarface*, but you're not Mr. Clean either."

Ditto said, "Yeah, Al Pacino sucked, making like he was Cuban. He shoulda stayed in the Italian lane."

"That fucking sucked. Worst Cuban accent I've ever heard. It was embarrassing for him and us Cubans. So what does your mother think you're doing? Are you supposed to be working for a company? Driving a cab? Running a hot dog stand wearing your G-string?"

Ditto looked Esteban in the eyes. "I told her I bought and was running a bagel store."

"Oh shit, Ditto. That's good. Why the fuck did you make up something like that? What do you know about running a bagel shop?" Esteban was beginning to sense something, and it bothered him.

"I told her I owned this shop."

"What? You told your mother you owned this shop? This shop?" Esteban's voice cracked as he stabbed a forefinger on the counter.

"Wait, wait, wait. Take a breath and just listen to me. She's only going to be here for one day, and then she's going to her brother's house in Boston. That's the favor I need from you, Esteban. She's going to come by the store, and I need you and everyone to make believe I own the store. It'll only be for a couple of hours."

Esteban rubbed his head. Game, set, match. "When is she supposed to stop by, Ditto?"

"She'll be coming around in a couple of hours."

Esteban turned away from Ditto and tried to gather his composure. He failed. "You're fucked-up. Jesus, Gustavo. How am I going to explain this to Maria and Miguel? You little shit. You think a little advance warning would have been appropriate? And on a Saturday? You are fucked-up. This request is fucked-up, and you put me in a bad fucking place, Gustavo!"

Ditto watched as Esteban calmed down and went into the back of the shop. Maria and Miguel figured something was up when Esteban gathered the employees in a scrum to inform them that they would be performing in a theater production directed by Ditto. With an eye on the front of the store—and Ditto—they listened to Esteban's pitch.

"Ditto is el jefe?" asked Pepe. "For two hours we are going to be working for him?"

"Yes, until his mother leaves," explained Esteban.

The employees exchanged confused looks, shrugged their shoulders, and said they'd go along with whatever Esteban asked them to do.

"How long is this really going to go on for?" asked Miguel unhappily.

"Not too long. An hour. Maybe an hour and a half."

Miguel and Maria looked at one another and

nodded their assent, but Esteban understood he was on his own to play game show host for Ditto's production.

"Ditto's mother might recognize me, and I have a lot of baking to get done, so I'm staying in the back," said Maria.

Miguel said, "She doesn't know me, but I'll be busy taking orders. Break a leg, Esteban."

Esteban returned to find Ditto looking out the window. "OK. Everyone is on board. One last thing—don't call me by my fucking name. Call me Pasqual or something. Even if there's only the smallest chance of it, I don't want your mom to recognize me."

"Yeah, yeah. Pasqual is good. Pasqual."

"Don't forget my name, you fucking runt. You owe me fucking big-time, Gustavo."

Ditto saw his mother approaching the store. "She's here! She's here! Get ready!" He quickly took his position behind the front counter while Esteban grudgingly went to the back of the shop.

"Mami! Mami!" Ditto warmly welcomed his mother with a big hug.

"My son, you look wonderful!"

Ditto enthusiastically escorted his mom as he showcased "his" store. Esteban hid in the background behind an apron and a hairnet, all the while watching the action in the shop and listening to Ditto's mom bestow praise. "Mijo! I am so proud of you! Look at this! At what you have done!"

Ditto was beaming as if he had just been told he was a new father, and proceeded to sit down at a table to enjoy a delightful bagel interlude with his mother.

"Gustavo, your father would be so proud of you. Most people thought you were a lost cause after you got arrested, but not me! Not your mami! I knew you would overcome all of that and become a success!"

"Mami, while you're here, let me treat you to lunch. When's tio coming to pick you up?"

"I told him to pick me up in an hour, mijo."

"Where are you going from here?"

"We are driving up to Tio's house in Boston."

Ditto was relieved to hear confirmation that she was Boston-bound. He nodded his head approvingly, then looked at the counter. He yelled, "Pasqual!" while waving Esteban over to the table.

Esteban slowly approached, cursing under his breath and communicating certain sentiments through his threatening stare at Ditto.

"Mami, this is Pasqual, one of our best employees. Tell him what you would like to eat."

"Mucho gusto, Pasqual. You look a little familiar. Where are you from?"

"Spain, señora."

"Aahh. You look Cuban. Is my handsome son, Gustavo, a good boss?"

Esteban glared at Ditto with glassy eyes and gurgled, "He is the best, señora."

Ditto leaned back in the chair, gleefully smiling at Esteban. "Tell him what you would like to eat, Mami."

"Bueno. I would like a café con leche and a couple of empanadas de carne."

As Esteban turned to go back to the kitchen and place the order, Ditto stopped him, saying, "Espera, Pasqual. I would like a western omelet, also with café con leche."

Esteban looked menacingly at Ditto and attempted to walk away again.

"Wait. Where are you going, papi? Put some

American cheese on it also, and extra hash browns. I'm hungry."

Esteban again attempted to return to the kitchen, and Ditto again stopped him in mid-step.

"Pasqual, aren't you going to ask me what kind of bread I want?"

Esteban turned to face Ditto, murmuring under his breath, but did not respond to his question.

"Let me have sourdough bread, toasted dark. And also a tres leches for us to share for dessert. Make it as fast as you can, because she has to leave soon. Thanks."

Esteban took a deeper-than-usual breath and rigidly strolled away, muttering in an unrecognizable language under his breath.

Ditto's mother leaned forward and commented, "Mijo, you say he's one of your best employees?"

"Sí, Mami."

"Well, I don't like him. You better be careful with him, because I don't think he likes you very much."

When the order was ready, Esteban gestured to Ditto to come get the food. Ditto shook his head disapprovingly, wanting Esteban to deliver the food to the table, but Esteban's patience with Ditto had expired, and he refused to budge from where the food was placed at the front counter. Esteban assertively signaled to Ditto to come get his order, concluding the gesture by flipping him the finger. Ditto, not wanting to waste any time, hustled to get the tray.

Esteban quietly warned him that this charade had to come to a conclusion. "Listen, dude. How much longer?"

"Half hour. Half hour. That's it. My uncle is coming to get her any minute. She'll eat and then we're done.

Please, just hold on for another thirty minutes."

"And listen, shithead. Don't fucking tell me to get anything else for you. This is all you're having!"

Ditto returned to the table, where they indulged in every morsel of food on the tray. Esteban saw that they had finished eating and asked one of his employees to go over and clean their table. He wanted to keep Ditto and his mom away from the front counter—and himself.

Ditto saw his uncle come into the shop. "Here's Tio, Mami." They cheerfully greeted her brother and proceeded to show him around the store too, including a brief chat with "Pasqual." After an exchange of pleasantries, Ditto's uncle congratulated him on turning his life around and wished him well. Although Ditto offered him some Cuban coffee, his uncle declined, stating that they had to get on the road to beat the rush-hour traffic.

As Ditto waved goodbye to his mom and uncle, Esteban took off his apron and reclaimed ownership of his store. However, he held on to the apron.

"Listen, Esteban, I can't thank you enough, bro. My mom thinks I'm her hero son. I think she's gonna put me back in her will. So what do you want, Esteban? Leave a five-hundred-dollar tip? Rent a table for the month?"

Esteban threw the apron at Ditto.

"What do you want me to do with this?"

"You're on cleanup duty for the next month, Gustavo."

"What? What are you talking about?"

"The store closes at four. You will start today, and also show up tomorrow, and every Saturday and Sunday at three p.m. for a month, and start cleaning the store before we shut down for the day. Just to be clear, you start today, and I mean today, at three p.m."

"What? C'mon, Esteban!"

"Wait, Gustavo. Was your mom proud of you for owning this store? Were you parading around like a peacock showing off 'your' store?"

"Yeah."

"And you treated me like your grunt as well, right?"

"I guess so."

"Then I want you to 'own' "—Esteban drew air quotes with both hands—"the store every Saturday and Sunday for a month and do what we do every day." Esteban crossed his arms. "That's not too much to ask for giving you guys lunch and renting you the store and my employees for an hour, is it, Gustavo-o-o-o-o?"

"I guess not."

"Then take your apron, and we'll see you later today. And you're welcome."

Three employees had overheard the conversation and sang in unison, "See you later, Ditto!" as he left the shop.

Saturday afternoon was waning, and at three p.m. Ditto walked through the front door of the shop. He was welcomed by a rousing round of applause by the employees, as if he were a conquering hero returning to his homeland. Ditto went to the back of the store and reluctantly tied on his apron (which needed to be folded in half to accommodate his height).

"Start him on the grill!" said Esteban.

One of the employees took Ditto by the elbow and escorted him to the grill, then demonstrated how the grease had to be completely drained into a bucket and then deposited into a special waste container. It was a disgusting endeavor, like tipping an outhouse on its side after it had been on a construction site for a week. Ditto began to gag. "Are you fucking kidding me?" The employee further explained that, after the grease was completely removed, Ditto had to scrub and polish the grill until it shone like the chrome on a vintage '57 Ford Thunderbird.

"When you're done, Mr. Ditto, I want to be able to see if I have any cavities in my mouth from the reflection."

It wasn't long before Ditto had an epiphany. These came naturally to him, an inherent trait that had earned him his reputation for scamming people. He concluded that, although he would show up to the shop every Saturday and Sunday and strap on an apron, he wouldn't clean anything; instead, he would pay each of the three employees fifty dollars to clean the store on his behalf. He also insisted that the money secure their silence. "Don't say a word about this to any of the bosses!"

Ditto threw his apron to the side and sat down near the window to watch the cleanup activities of the employees he'd paid to do his job, while he snacked on a sandwich and chips and conducted his business affairs. His mami would have been proud. He had once again become the proprietor-in-chief of the store.

CHAPTER 11

In which Ditto finds a former friend from the neighborhood is muscling in on his business and Maria and Rosa come to Ditto's rescue.

"What the fuck are you doing, asshole!? He's my client! He's my mark! You know that! Get the fuck away from my people and stay on your side of the state, motherfucker!"

Maria came out from the rear of the shop. It was a typical slow Monday morning, and other than Ditto frantically pacing and shouting into his phone, the store was empty.

"That's right, asshole. Yeah, yeah, just show up here and see what happens!" Ditto angrily shoved his phone into his jacket.

"Ditto, what was that all about? I've never seen you this pissed off."

"Maria, this piece of shit Julio—"

Maria bristled at the mention of Julio. "Julio? You don't mean Julio Costa, do you?"

"That's exactly who I mean."

"No question he's a piece of shit, Ditto. Do you remember when his mother's jewelry went missing, and the whole neighborhood knew, and he denied having anything to do with it? Then he buys a new car a week later. He's trouble. He's sold drugs, has gotten busted like six times, served some time, and was always hanging out with the shit of the shit in the neighborhood. This guy is disgusting, and he treats his mother like mierda."

Julio Costa's family DNA for criminal activity was well known to the Fernandez family and the neighborhood at large. He was raised in a broken home by an itinerant alcoholic father who beat up his wife and whored around with other women. Julio's older sister, Consuelo, at sixteen stole a car with some friends and held up a convenience store. She threatened the store clerk with a fake revolver. The cops caught up with her when someone in the neighborhood ratted her out for a five-hundred-dollar reward. Consuelo got off lightly with probation because she was a juvenile. She ended up running away from home when she was seventeen with a guy who was thirty. She was never seen again, but she had left her mark on her impressionable younger brother. And then Julio met Ditto.

"I know, Maria. He used to be a friend. When we were young, the Cuban guys had us two running around for them collecting money."

"Wait, you were actually friends with him? I thought you guys just kinda knew each other, but never ran around together."

"Yup. We were more like work friends and that was it—until he started a little side hustle and started selling drugs. He hit on all of the Cuban guys' customers."

"Gustavo, everyone knew he was dealing drugs

but figured he was working for the Cubans."

"Exactly! That's why the Cubans got pissed off. People thought *they* were the ones dealing, but they didn't want anything to do with drugs. Drugs would have put too much of a light on their activities. They just wanted to control the loans, gambling, and whores."

Esteban had walked in and caught what Ditto said. He confirmed the story. "Julio was a nasty little weasel who was pretending to be like fucking Scarface. He was hanging out with a bunch of lowlifes that thought they were like Hells Angels, but when shit got real, they scampered off into corners, kinda like roaches when you switch on a light. And like roaches, it was hard to get rid of them, so you just dealt with them."

"So what happened to him?" asked Maria.

"The Cubans brought him in, worked him over, cut him loose, and warned him to stop dealing drugs. Then the fucker told those guys that I was doing it as well."

"I know you never dealt drugs, Gustavo."

"I know, and so do the Cubans. They didn't buy his bullshit. He wanted to fuck me up as well, the motherfucker. But they knew. The same way they knew to call him out for dealing. These guys rule the streets and they have people everywhere. Including cops."

"So what happened to him then?" pushed Maria.

Esteban jumped into the conversation. "He kept selling coke and then started doing loans at the same time."

"The same thing the Cubans did with their loan business?"

"Yup. Fucking unbelievable, right? Just asking for

it," responded Ditto. "The Cubans warned him again and told him it was the last time."

"Is that when he left town?" Maria was consumed with curiosity.

Esteban picked up the story. "He hung around for like six months, laying low, and what finally forced him to leave was that he had a kid with his girlfriend. The kid was still an infant when he ran out on them like his pants were on fire. A1 legitimate asshole. He cut all ties with everyone in the neighborhood, so his girlfriend never knew where he went. I suspect she hasn't seen a cent from him."

Ditto jumped in. "Julio moved about a hundred miles upstate, where he partnered with some hayseeds to provide the same gray market loans he was peddling here. The only problem is, the return on investment there is not at the same level that the hood rats from the inner-city streets are getting."

"And one hundred miles isn't far enough," Esteban said. "It's like the pesky squirrel in the attic. It has to be caught and relocated many, many miles away so it doesn't find its way back." Esteban went into storytelling mode. "I had a squirrel problem once at the house."

"I remember that," said Maria.

Ditto asked, "So what did you do?"

"I asked a friend what I had to do to get rid of a squirrel in my attic, and he told me he had a Havahart rodent trap he would lend me. He had squirrels in his attic too. He told me that squirrels have an incredible sense of their environment and a huge attachment to their home base. That they have a biological homing device. An internal GPS. Like salmon swimming back to spawn. He said after you capture a tree rat, you have to drive at least five, not a couple, miles away, and let it loose."

"Get the fuck out of here, Esteban. I didn't think you had to go that far away," objected Ditto.

"Yup, that's what he said. So I asked him how you get the squirrel in the trap. He told me it's simple: Put some food on the trigger inside the hatch, put the trap in the attic, and wait for the sound of the trap being sprung. Then, he said, after the squirrel is in the cage, you fill your bathtub with water."

Maria looked confused. "Fill up a bathtub?"

"That makes no sense," said Ditto.

"After the tub is full, you drop the Havahart in the water and drown the squirrel."

"What? He drowned a squirrel?" Maria exclaimed.

Ditto started to laugh uncontrollably. "Is that what you did? Fuck. That's beautiful. Squirrel-icide."

"No, Ditto. I drove the squirrel out beyond city limits and let it loose. As I was getting ready to release it, I saw that it only had one eye."

Ditto looked incredulous. "Only one eye?"

"Yeah. It looked like a pirate squirrel. I walked a good half mile into the woods, opened the cage, and let him loose. I wished him well in what I thought would be his new home."

"You *thought*?" asked a confused-looking Ditto.

Maria picked up the story. "Two weeks later, Miguel and me were at Esteban's, and we heard this noise in the attic. It was something scrambling around, like a squirrel. Which it was."

Esteban interjected, "But not just any squirrel. It was the same fucking squirrel."

Ditto responded cynically, "Get the fuck outta here, Esteban. How could it have been the same squirrel?"

"Well, Ditto, I put the Havahart up there and caught it again. The biggest clue was that the same fucking eye was missing. It was the same squirrel.

Incredible. But this time, I drove it out like ten miles, and we never saw it again."

"Holy shit!"

"So, Ditto, I think that's what happened in this case with Julio. A hundred miles wasn't far enough to go, and the dude found his way back. Like the squirrel."

"He moved back permanently?" asked Maria.

Ditto became animated. "No, no. He just comes down two, three times a week, trying to do some business loaning money. He's fucking with my business and going after my clients, and I need to get his ass outta here."

"Does his ex-girlfriend know he's back in town?" Maria posed this question already knowing the answer, using it as a tactic to set up a Machiavellian suggestion.

"Nah. He would not want this to be public knowledge. No way she knows he's in town. Otherwise, he wouldn't be here doing this bullshit."

Maria maintained her gaze on Ditto, and Esteban realized what she was thinking. He, too, looked at Ditto, waiting for a glimmer of creative thought.

Ditto finally broke the silence. "Why are both of you looking at me?" Then the penny dropped. "Wait! If she knew he was around, she would chase his ass."

Ditto had achieved a state of enlightenment that revealed a simple and elegant solution for him *and* the jilted girlfriend in dealing with their common nemesis.

"Exactly, Ditto. And you won't have to resort to even a minor form of unnecessary force." Maria detested violence.

Esteban laughed and said, "He'll be out of here so quick, he'll leave skid marks."

"OK. I have to find out where Julio's girlfriend is. The trick is going to be getting her and the boy and Julio in the same relative jurisdiction."

Ditto looked around thoughtfully. "Maybe this shop. Zat OK?"

"Go for it, Ditto. You have our blessing," responded Maria, as Esteban nodded approvingly.

Several days passed. Maria, Esteban, and Miguel had not heard from or seen Ditto. He had seemingly gone AWOL. But they did see Julio. He would pop into the shop a couple of times a week and meet with a diverse range of people. If he was at all concerned about seeing Ditto, he didn't show it. But Maria and Esteban expected the day to inevitably come when an impromptu fireworks display would entertain the customers. And the fuse was lit on a particular day at nine thirty in the morning when a mother with a young child entered the shop and approached the front counter.

"Hi. Can I help you?" asked Esteban, who suddenly felt an unexpected twinge of anxiety.

"Just a cup of coffee and an orange juice. What kinds of muffins do you have?"

"What do you like? All our muffins were made fresh this morning."

"Blueberry?"

"Blueberry muffin sounds like the one!"

"Thank you."

Esteban glanced at the boy, who looked like Julio. That simultaneously confirmed his suspicions and raised his blood pressure.

"Would you like the muffin toasted and buttered, or just toasted, or just buttered?"

"Thank you, no. I'll take it just like that. Thanks."

The woman grabbed the boy's hand and led him to a table in the back corner, where she had a clear view of the front door. She sat patiently while keeping her son entertained with paper and crayons.

An hour and a couple of refills later, Esteban was looking out the front window when he saw Julio coming through the parking lot kitty-corner to the shop. Julio strolled through the front door and greeted Esteban at the front counter. "What's up, Esteban? Let me have the usual. Café con leche and a Cuban sandwich, dude. I'll be over there where that guy is."

Julio joined an apparent business associate at the front window. That's when Esteban caught sight of Ditto outside the shop, trying to conceal himself behind a forlorn tree in a planter. The only thing he was missing was camouflage attire.

Esteban felt obliged to test his theory that the woman was Julio's former girlfriend, and the boy his son. The woman had taken her son to the restroom and was unaware of Julio's presence. When she returned, Esteban cleared his throat and hurled a yell toward him. "Julio!" Then, twice as loud, "JULIO!"

"Sí, Esteban. What's up?"

"Does your friend there want anything, JULIO?"

The woman stirred and, with her son in hand, walked up to the front counter. She seemed intent on affirming beyond a doubt that this was the Julio who had long neglected his obligations as a father and husband. She was fueled by four years of pent-up contempt, and Esteban could feel her rising temperature radiating in her periphery. Julio looked in Esteban's direction. His eyes reflected a five-alarm fire, and he was biting his bottom lip so hard that a spot of blood appeared.

"Julio!!!" The woman let out an eardrum-shattering scream, and Julio catapulted from his chair and stood bolt upright. She followed with a barrage of select modifiers. "¡Hijo de puta! You motherfucker!"

"Yolanda?"

"That's right. It's me, you worthless piece of shit! Four years later! And this is your son, cabrón."

Julio's associate did not want any part of the festivities and sprinted out the door.

"Yeah, you go. Now it's just us three, you fuck!"

Julio, visibly shaken, turned white, turned around, and threw up.

Esteban interceded. "You can't do this in here. Take it somewhere else, please."

"Julio, you better be ready to make up for lost time! You disappear and show up here! I can't believe it!"

Esteban directed one of the employees to clean up the slop while he gently escorted them out of the shop.

"I am sorry, Esteban …"

"No, no. No need to worry, Julio, and good luck."

The following week brought no sign of Ditto, and Julio had apparently decided to relocate his business address.

"Man, I wish I could have seen that mother and child and MIA husband reunion," hummed Miguel.

"Trust me, you didn't want to be here," Esteban said. "You should have seen Julio. His balls were skewered with a hot knife, bro. What a sight."

Maria changed the tone of the conversation. "That's not nice, Esteban. It's kind of tragic. I mean, how would you feel if that was your kid? By the way, has anyone seen or heard from Ditto?"

"Nope," replied Esteban.

"Me neither," said Miguel.

"Don't you think that's strange, Esteban? I mean,

for him not to come around, especially with Julio disappearing. I have a lot of questions. The whole thing was staged, but how?"

It was almost closing time when Ditto came into the shop. "HELLO, MY PEOPLE! How's my people doing?! I'm baaaack!"

"Ditto!" Miguel yelled. "Where the fuck have you been, dude?"

Esteban joined the chorus. "Yeah, where the fuck have you been?"

Ditto demonstrated some fancy footwork, singing, "I've been taking care of business …"

Everyone burst out laughing.

"Julio is dust. He's a footnote in the pages of my biography. And, Maria, I owe it all to *you*!" He applauded her as he said, "That was una idea increible."

Maria smiled. "Thanks, Ditto. And you know he's gone for sure?"

"Well, he's not 'gone' gone, but he's done and done. D-o-n-e, done."

"What happened with his girlfriend and their son?" asked Esteban.

"Julio is staying here with them. He ain't goin' back to whitelandia. He'll be slumming it in the spic jungle."

"I don't understand, Ditto," said Maria.

"Look, what happened was, the girl was not going to let him go back upstate, and if he did want to go back, Julio was going to have to take her and the kid with him—*and* her mother! Then the rest of the girl's family also got into it, and sadly Julio is now looking for an alternate and less colorful career path."

"He knows people with influence in this town and will probably get a job with the city so he can get benefits," observed Esteban.

"But how'd you pull all this together, Ditto?" Maria couldn't wait to hear how Ditto had executed her idea.

"It wasn't easy. It started by accident, really, because after you said what you said, Maria, I happened to go out with some friends and a distant cousin I hadn't seen for years. Maria, have you ever met my cousin Rosa? My aunt Brenda's daughter."

Maria shrugged. "I don't think so."

"Well, she's a couple of years younger than Julio's girlfriend, Yolanda, but both are from the same neighborhood. We're having dinner and I bring up this bullshit, and how this guy Julio had come back to town and was fucking around with my business. Rosa had never met Julio, but for a time she lived a couple of blocks from Yolanda and knew the story, him running off and shit. She said he was a real douchebag, leaving her like that with a baby."

"OK, but hurry it up, Ditto," said Maria.

"I agreed with Rosa that he's a douchebag and piled on, describing the shit he was trying to pull on me, *and* on top of it not telling his ex he was back in town. Then my cousin volunteered a suggestion. She told me she sees Yolanda almost every day because they work in the same office building. Then, without me asking her, she said next time she ran across Yolanda, she would start some small talk with her, and when Julio was brought up in conversation, Rosa would inform her of Julio's habit of visiting a certain bagel shop."

"Oh my God. Gold. You couldn't have planned it better. So that's why Yolanda showed up here."

"Correct, Maria. Rosa ran into Yolanda and told her."

Maria continued, "You see, Ditto. God is looking out for you. God intervened."

"He did intervene, Maria. First with your idea, then my cousin's strategy. I honestly hope it works out for Julio—you know, walking the straight and narrow. He would have never been successful in this racket. He was going to end up dead, so in a strange way, God intervened for him as well."

Ditto's phone rang. "Oh shit. This is a guy that needed money and Julio had hit him up ..." Ditto gave a thumbs-up as he left to discuss business with his new customer.

The three Cubans congratulated one another with *attaboys* at having contributed to Ditto's comeback, knowing they had secured customer loyalty that would endure for the life of the bagel shop.

Maria's eyes fell on the tip jar they kept on the front counter, and she noticed something unusual—a white envelope. She opened it to find a note from Ditto, along with five hundred-dollar bills and four tickets to a Broadway musical. She texted Ditto: "Oye, thank you very much for the five hundred dollars and the tickets to my favorite Broadway musical. I've been wanting to see this show for a while. The employees will appreciate the money—we're giving all of it to them—but we'll enjoy *Chicago*."

Soon Ditto sent a reply: "Because of you and the crew, I'm back in business and will be hanging out at the shop a lot more. Your help meant a lot. I plan on spending a lot of time at the store, and hope you don't get sick of me. Thank you for your friendship and support."

Maria showed the text to Miguel and Esteban.

"That's cute, but does this mean he's going to become part of the furniture here?" asked Esteban.

"Looks that way, Esteban," said Maria.

Esteban looked at her. "Then charge him rent."

Chapter 12

In which Esteban, Maria, and Miguel open the shop and their hearts when disaster strikes.

It was ten p.m. on a windy summer's night and Miguel was thinking the very same thing as Maria.

"Miguel! Do you smell that? Where's that coming from?" she anxiously cried out.

Maria was particularly sensitive to the distinctive odor of smoke, and for a couple of reasons: It related to the old expression "where there's smoke, there's fire," but it also was due to a painful reminder of how she had witnessed family homes located in a predominantly Puerto Rican neighborhood by the New Jersey waterfront burned to the ground one summer. Although the area was composed of run-down tenements, this neighborhood was prime real estate, located as it was on the shores of the Hudson River, which offered breathtaking views of Manhattan and convenient access for commuters. Over the course of several years, real estate developers had aggressively purchased dilapidated properties in this neighborhood, and the only way they were going to be able to recoup their investment was to gentrify the community, which meant driving out the current residents, whom the developers considered financially uninspiring.

The continual, seemingly daily fires spanned over the course of the summer, and this season became known as "the summer of matches." The suspicion on the street was that these fires were acts of arson to drive people out. New construction would attract higher rents and a white-collar working class. Over time, the area was being transformed into one of the most expensive stretches of residential neighborhoods in New Jersey.

Miguel looked out the window and noticed windblown black particles drifting in the air. Maria threw on a sweatshirt as Miguel rushed to the front door. She joined him on the porch.

"Oh my God, Miguel! What is that? What's going on?"

Neighbors were gathering on the street. "This shit is ashes. It's raining ashes. Something is burning pretty hot and it must be close. Let's walk to the bluff and look around."

Miguel and Maria were joined by other anxious neighbors. As everyone peered over the cliffs overlooking the neighborhood along the river, they were unprepared for the sight of billowing black smoke and an area engulfed in an orange and yellow glow.

Someone yelled, "Man, that looks like the Burning Man festival in Nevada!" Not everyone understood their neighbor's metaphor.

Miguel and Maria left the spectators and headed for their car. Miguel wanted to confirm the location of the fire, because he was concerned about the size of the blaze and its proximity to the bagel shop. They drove farther north along the cliffs in an attempt to get a better view, but found the streets closed off by the police. They had to park the car and continue on foot, and what they witnessed was disconcerting. The firefighters were spraying copious amounts of water on the rooftops of homes located on the edge of the cliff so that the roofs would not ignite from the swarm of hot embers circulating in the blustery night air. The bagel shop was in the neighborhood below the cliff and was potentially in the literal line of fire.

People who had been evacuated from their homes stood helplessly by, watching the apocalyptic nightmare that was unfolding in front of them. Miguel and Maria decided they needed to get to the shop and determine if it was at risk. Maria called Esteban, who had just gone to bed. "Listen. There's a huge fire going on by the store. We're gonna try to get down there. We're in the car, trying to find a way down."

Esteban groggily responded, "Shit. OK, Maria. I'm on my way."

The sound of emergency vehicle sirens inundated the night air as multiple municipalities responded to the five-alarm fire. Miguel managed to carefully navigate through what was now the barely recognizable maze of roads he knew like the back of his hand, while swerving around emergency vehicles, until they got within three blocks of the shop. As they hurried through the streets, they caught their first sight of the shop, and what they saw took their breath away.

The area surrounding the strip mall where the bagel shop was located had transformed into a scene from a disaster movie: Smoke from the fire was obscuring the night sky, and the proximate streets were absent of people going about their normal routines, replaced with emergency personnel responding to the blaze and taking care of displaced, panicked residents. As Maria and Miguel got closer to the shop, they felt the heat radiating from a frenzied, twenty-five-foot-high wall of fire that was in the process of rapidly consuming connected rows of wood-framed homes down the block. They were able to make their way through throngs of people, scattered equipment, and a pervasive mist produced by a mixture of smoke and moisture resulting from the hoses spraying water on the blaze, and proceeded to open the shop. Miguel flicked the lights on and was relieved that the electricity was still flowing.

"Miguel, we have to do something for these people. Go out there and start telling the first responders that they are welcome to use the shop as a way station for patients or residents, and they can get all the food and water they need here."

As Maria bustled around the shop, Miguel hustled outside. He saw Esteban and shouted, "She's inside!"

Esteban burst into the shop. "Maria, I can't believe this. It's an inferno out there. What are we doing?"

"Esteban, we're opening the shop and helping everyone out there. Miguel is trying to get the word out."

"Wait, Maria. What are we talking about? You mean you want to give away all of our food? That's thousands of dollars we're going to lose tonight. You sure you want to do this?"

Esteban was mentally computing the monetary losses related to giving away all the food from the shop.

"What's wrong with you, Esteban? You can't put money in front of a tragedy! This is a tragedy!"

"Maria, giving away all our food is also a tragedy— for us!"

As if on cue, the door to the shop abruptly swung

open and several EMS personnel tumbled in, settling on some chairs and catching their breath. Esteban immediately realized the situation was desperate. "You guys alright? What do you need? Water, coffee, food, crumb cake? Anything you want."

The EMS crew simply requested water and expressed humble appreciation for the gesture, but Esteban and Maria nonetheless responded with water, pastries, and chips, and then Maria said, "I've got coffee going now. It'll be ready in a couple of minutes. Sandwiches are coming."

Maria approached them and quietly asked, "How are you guys doing? How bad is it?"

One of the crew members lifted her head from her hands, sat up, and responded, "We're OK, considering. I've never seen anything like this, anywhere around here. That fire spread so fast. Homes were just lighting up like matchsticks for blocks."

An older responder gasped, "They're all wood homes. The flames spread like a wildfire."

Maria continued to probe. "Were people able to get out?"

"Yeah, amazingly, as far as we can tell, everyone was able to get out. But they left with nothing on their backs. No time."

Miguel came through the door, leading an ensemble of people, including residents and more first responders, into the shop.

"There's water over there, coffee over there," he said, pointing to the items. "Grab chips over there and anything else you guys want. No charge. Please make yourselves at home."

"Thank you for everything. We've got to get back."

It was now two a.m., and even though they had been active in the field for two and a half hours, the crew had found refuge for a total of fifteen minutes in an attempt to gain a third or possibly fourth wind in their ongoing commitment to helping people.

"Be safe out there. Thank you for everything." Maria waved goodbye to the crew as they returned to the mayhem taking place outside, and welcomed more newcomers to the shop. Maria and Esteban prepared cold-cut sandwiches as Miguel fired up the grill and started putting together egg and cheese sandwiches.

People kept coming in to find sanctuary. The threesome, fueled by adrenaline, worked through the night, catering to the demands of the emergency situation. By four in the morning, the fire finally subsided, thanks to the heroic efforts of the firefighters, who had managed to contain the blaze, which had consumed the fuel that fed it. The bagel shop had been saved.

Officials informed the three owners that the shop could remain open, and Esteban called the employees and told them they were to show up for work. Access to the area by car was restricted, but that didn't matter to the bagel roller and baker, as they always rode their bikes to work. Pepe had actually shown up at his regular time, three thirty, to be greeted by a shop full of people and first responders. Miguel explained to Pepe what had happened overnight, and that the shop had been open since eleven thirty.

Pepe leapt in and began preparing and baking bagels, especially for the wholesale customers, who would expect to be able to pick up their orders. At five a.m., the police had opened up a trickle of street traffic, prompting Esteban to contact the wholesale customers in case they wondered about access to the shop.

At precisely five o'clock, Emil, the bagel shop gigolo, walked into the shop. "Jefe, is everyone OK?"

"Emil, all these homes burned. No one died, though, so that's a blessing."

The sun rose, exposing an apocalyptic field of charred, smoldering debris, and streets still partially covered with what looked like a snake pit of fire hoses. Toxic plumes of smoke slowly rose into the air.

Esteban, like his sister and brother-in-law, didn't have another ounce of energy to spare, but they still had not finished helping out. Maria baked pastries, Pepe baked bagels, and Miguel was waiting for the fresh bagels so he could start making breakfast sandwiches again.

Esteban, who was gathering food items to take to the people at the local recreation center, continued, "Emil, no joke. Maria, Miguel, and me have been here since eleven thirty last night. We've been up all night …"

"Jefe, I was up all night also."

"You feeling OK?"

"Sí, sí. I was up all night with Señora Cohen."

"Mrs. Cohen? The Jewish lady that always gets a pound of whitefish, cranberry tuna, and flagels delivered?"

"Sí. It was my last delivery yesterday, and I left her house this morning. She drinks Pepsi for breakfast."

Miguel overheard the conversation and wanted to confirm what he had heard. "Emil, dude. She's like twenty years older than you and weighs like two hundred pounds. What the fuck were you doin' all night? I hope it was cooking for her and nothing else. There's no way. No, no, no. In fact, I don't want to hear any more!"

"Jefe, her husband die, and she is lonely lady, but

she don't act like an old lady. She was de one on fire last night, and me, I was de fireman."

Astonished, Miguel responded, "You were what? The fireman?"

"Sí. I put her fire out. It took all night, but I take out my fire hose and take care of it."

Esteban and Miguel were shaking their heads in disbelief, and laughing under their breath, as Emil continued to add to his legendary status as the bagel shop gigolo. "And she tip me twenty dollars for de delivery. I like the whitefish. I never have it before. Es bueno."

"Well, I'm not going to be able to look at her or take her order now, because I might say something stupid like 'Would you like a side of Emil with your order?'" said Miguel, eliciting a burst of laughter from Emil.

"Or maybe, Emil, the shop should do a promotional centerfold calendar with all of our male employees, with you featured on the front cover. Like firehouses do with their firemen."

Emil was grinning ear to ear and nodding affirmatively at Miguel's suggestion.

"Forget it, Emil. I am kidding. I'm grossed out, thank you very much."

Esteban ignored the banter, yelling out, "Emil, do us a favor, please. Don't bring that shit up again, and grab all of this stuff and take it over to the recreation center. There are some hungry people over there!"

This philanthropic activity continued for a couple more days, until such time as the first responders and the residents insisted on paying for the food that was delivered, including generous tips for the employees.

• • •

One afternoon, three days later, Mrs. Cohen personally came into the shop to order her usual basket of delights, which now included Emil. Miguel was surprised to see her in the store and quickly went to the back, calling for Esteban's attention. Mrs. Cohen was dressed strikingly differently, sporting an ensemble displaying more color and flair than in past visits. She poked around the shop as if she were looking for a specific something—or rather, someone.

Miguel advised Emil of Mrs. Cohen's presence and instructed him to take her order. When she saw Emil, Mrs. Cohen beamed a never-ending grin, as if she were looking at a mythological being or a Salvadorian god. Emil, the Salvadorian delivery god. Miguel wondered whether Emil would enjoy Pepsi for breakfast the next morning.

The compassion exhibited by the three Cubans in helping the first responders and the displaced residents through the night of the devastating fire endeared Maria, Miguel, and Esteban to their neighbors and forever wove the shop and its owners into the fabric of the community they served.

Chapter 13

In which Maria's attractive friend finds favor in an exclusive country club and Esteban resumes his spy skills at a Shiva to find a top-secret rugelach recipe.

"What time is it? Oh shit. Hurry up! Hurry up, Maria. We have to get to the club."

Maria was attentively putting the finishing touches on her makeup. "What is the rush, Miguel? If we're a little late, they can have a drink at the bar and wait a little bit."

"Maria, you know we have to be at the club to greet them."

"Miguel, you need to calm down. It's not like we're having dinner with royalty. It's just Victor, Beatrice, and Ithañia. They'll understand." Ithañia and Maria had been friends since childhood.

Real or imagined, Miguel's sense of urgency arose from the fact that he and Maria were members of a private country club, and on admission had been advised that they were only the second Hispanic couple at the club since it was established more than seven decades ago. It seemed obvious to Maria and

Miguel that their off-white complexion was as brown as the club membership committee wanted to extend their color palette in their quest to be multiracially inclusive. The other Hispanic couple apparently descended from regal European bloodlines, with skin coloration as white as a physician's lab coat.

But the matter confronting Maria and Miguel now was a bit more complicated because Victor was Black and his wife, Beatrice, was a white-skinned Cuban woman, while Ithañia was an assertive, dark-skinned Puerto Rican female business professional. To date, Blacks had not broken the club's racial barrier.

Victor was a highly regarded orthopedic surgeon who had gotten his medical degree from Cornell, while Beatrice had graduated from Stanford and was CFO of a Fortune 100 corporation. Ithañia had her educational chops affirmed with diplomas from Princeton and the Wharton School of Business, and owned and operated, along with her parents, several highly regarded and successful restaurants.

Maria disregarded the ignorant stereotypes (because she was a stereotype herself) and was innocently ambivalent to the circumstances. Nonetheless, Miguel took all the precautions needed to ensure his guests weren't placed in an uncomfortable position where they would feel the slightest bit of unease because of an indelicate, intentional or unintentional, breakdown of mannerly decorum. Consequently, he wanted everyone to enter the dining room in unison. As they weaved in and out of traffic and ignored yellow lights, Miguel asked Maria to call their guests and casually suggest that the seven p.m. reservation was flexible and they needn't rush.

"No. I'm not calling them. We'll see them when we get there."

"Is Esteban meeting us at the club or are we picking him up?" asked an anxious Miguel.

"He isn't joining us for dinner."

"Why not? He hasn't seen Victor or Beatrice in a while."

"No. He's gone to the hospital."

"To the hospital? I didn't hear anything about this. Is he in the ER? Is he OK? Why are we going to dinner instead of being with Esteban?"

"Slow down, Miguel. There's nothing wrong with him. He's visiting Harvey."

"Harvey Muskowitz?"

"Yes. He's there now."

"Harvey Muskowitz—the Royal Rugelach Man?"

"One and the same, Miguel."

"What's wrong with Harvey?"

Maria despondently responded, "He's actually dying."

"Dying? Whaddya mean dying? How could he be dying? I just saw him two days ago."

"Esteban heard that he's apparently on his deathbed."

"How the fuck did that happen?"

"We'll find out more after we hear from Esteban, Miguel."

"I don't mean to sound insensitive, but what's going to happen to his business? Where are we gonna get our rugelach? You know, Maria, I heard rumors that he had a journal that had all his secret recipes for making rugelach."

"I've heard that as well."

"Do you think it's true?"

"I *know* it is."

"How do you know?"

"Because he told me."

"He told you? Why would he tell you that?"

"I was laying out some filo dough one day, and I'm spreading butter on it, and he was delivering an order and saw me. He came over and asked me what I was going to bake, and he told me to add more vanilla here, and a little bit more cinnamon and sugar over there …"

"Were you making rugelach?"

"No, I wasn't, but because of his reputation as a great baker, I asked him how he knows so much. He said, 'Because I write everything down in my cooking journal. All my recipes are in my book.' He also said that he had recipes in his book, like for babka, that he hasn't even experimented with yet. Then he just smiled mysteriously and wandered away."

"Wow, Maria. That's interesting. That recipe book is gold. If we could get our hands on that, we could start a whole other line of business. You should have flirted with him."

Maria looked at Miguel with a punishing stare for suggesting she flirt with another man.

"I didn't, wouldn't, and now it's too late anyway, because he's going to die in the next couple of days, so forget about it."

"Maybe we could buy the recipe book from him? Whaddya think?"

Maria sighed.

When they arrived at the club, the valet, who happened to be Hispanic, informed them that their guests had arrived and had been directed to wait for them in the dining room bar. As they entered the club, Maria was genuinely filled with excitement to see their friends, while Miguel had to choke back his gastric reflux and calm his pulse rate. At the bar,

Miguel was happy to see their guests engaged in a jovial conversation with the bartender, and he relaxed, although he noticed that their group had attracted an abundance of interest and curiosity from many members.

Ithañia enthusiastically greeted Maria, "Muchacha, where you been?" After everyone exchanged the traditional Hispanic welcoming hugs and kisses, they toasted to the evening. Miguel trepidatiously asked if they had been received appropriately when they arrived, which prompted a round of positive affirmation by the three guests.

The evening was progressing enjoyably, but the ambience felt a bit subdued for the five Latinos. "This is all nice and sophisticated and stuff, but look around," commented Victor. He continued, "The average age in this place kind of feels like a nursing home. It's like a Medicare convention."

Maria interjected, "No doubt it takes a little getting used to. When we went home after the first time having dinner here, I felt like I had aged ten years from geriatric osmosis."

"This band is pretty interesting," said Beatrice as she pretended to yawn. "Does the band take requests, Maria?" Maria looked at Beatrice quizzically before she understood she was being teased. "Because some danzón music would be eminently livelier than Lawrence Welk."

Short of demonstrating her salsa moves by dancing on the table, Ithañia decided to inject some energy accelerant into the atmosphere. "OK, what kind of shots do you guys want? Tequila, vodka, what?" Everyone at the table responded with different answers, prompting Ithañia to conclude, "OK, tequila shots all 'round!"

Ithañia was a beautiful Puerto Rican girl with an athletic figure, long hair, smooth Caribbean skin, a precocious smile, and bewitching hazel eyes. As she approached the bar, Miguel noticed that it was bustling in its usual manner with a collection of historical artifacts, otherwise known as old codgers, enjoying a predinner cocktail. The bar had been divided in the traditional "old-school" gender groups, where one side was staked out by a group of elderly men while the other side was filled with a gaggle of their marital counterparts. The cultural composition of the assembled bone field suggested an avid constituency of a foregone Italian society, one that was emblematic of Martin Scorsese movies.

Ithañia reached the bar and leaned forward to engage with the bartender as the men clumsily jockeyed for position around her. "Let me have five tequila shots, please."

"Five tequila shots? Wow! That's some party you have going on there!" commented one of the Italian fossils. Others nodded in unison. None could take their eyes off the beautiful apparition that had so unexpectedly graced their otherwise uneventful night out.

Ithañia decided to have some fun. "Yes. Thank you. We like to have a good time."

Ithañia's comment was designed to elicit a predictable response, which, naturally, was uttered: "And we like to have a good time as well!"

"You really have beautiful eyes," observed one member of the hopelessly horny group, while another capitalized on a momentary spark of fortitude to ask, "What's your name?"

By now the lively interaction had been noticed by the wives, who began to make threatening eye contact with their spouses.

"My name is Ithañia," she responded, tilting a little to the front and flashing a mesmerizing smile.

"Ithañia? What an exotic name," gushed one of the men, while another added, "And what part of Italy are you from, Ithañia?"

Ithañia leaned in closer, murmured a few words, and then departed the circle of admiring glances with a "Good night, gentlemen." And with that, she returned to the table with the shots.

Maria offered a toast. "It's wonderful to be with dear friends tonight." She quietly added, "And I also want to toast to Ithañia's new fan club."

Beatrice amusedly asked, "What in the heck were you talking about with those men?"

"It was just a bunch of harmless old horny Italian men. They were cute."

"Their old ladies better watch out for them tonight," offered Victor. "You just reignited whatever is left of their libidos!"

Maria added, "You should have seen their old ladies. They looked pissed! In fact, they should be thanking you instead of being jealous, because you set up their old men for some action later tonight!"

"To us, and Ithañia!" exclaimed Victor as they raised their glasses.

Ithañia chuckled. "They asked me my name and what part of Italy was I from."

"What part of Italy you were from? They thought you were Italian?" questioned Miguel. "What did you tell them?"

"I winked at them and said, 'Mi amor, I'm from the PUERTO RICAN PART OF ITALY, BABY!'"

Miguel cheered and asked, "Another round?"

• • •

Esteban was at the shop when Miguel and Maria strolled in at eight a.m.

"You guys look hungover," said Esteban.

"Yes, we are indeed. Maria's friend Ithañia came with us to dinner, and she certainly moved the needle there a bit," responded a groggy Miguel.

"Sheesh. Ithañia? She's a handful, that woman, but she's a lot of fun. How're are you faring, my dear sister?"

"Esteban, all I know is that the older I get, the less alcohol I can drink and the earlier I want to go to sleep. What is the news about Harvey?"

"He passed away. Sad. He was admitted to the hospital and less than twenty-four hours later, he died."

Dismayed, Maria leaned on the counter to balance herself. "Oh my God, that's terrible. He was such a nice man. Always talked about the traveling they were going to do. What did he die from?"

"A heart attack. They thought they had stabilized him, to the point that they let in a couple of visitors. I was one of them and got to visit with him for a couple of minutes. Then, when I got home, I got a call from a friend telling me he had a second heart attack and died. Just like that. So, it's good you guys had a good time last night …"

"And what's going to happen to his business?" asked Miguel.

"His business? I asked my friend that same question, and he told me that Harvey's wife is going to sell it to a couple of investors that approached Harvey and made them a nice offer just months ago."

"Why don't we buy it?" asked Maria.

"It's not worth it. We have our hands full with our shop, and it's a whole other line of business."

"So we'll just keep buying the rugelach from the new owners, Esteban?"

"Well, I don't think so, because we don't have any allegiance to the new owners. We don't know them, and Harvey is gone now."

"So are we going to shop around for rugelach? Because our customers buy a lot of rugelach and we have to keep it in stock."

Miguel asked, "Won't it hurt Harvey's old lady if we don't buy from her?"

"No. We'll keep buying from her until she sells the business, and then we'll just make our own rugelach."

Maria's head snapped up. "What do you mean, 'make our own rugelach'? How can we make rugelach that would be as good as Harvey's?"

"Maria, could you make the rugelach if you had Harvey's recipes?"

"Harvey's recipes?" whispered Miguel.

"Yeah, Harvey's recipes. Yes. Maria, if we had Harvey's recipes, could you make them?"

"I suppose I could, but I don't have Harvey's recipes. Only Harvey has the recipes, and no one knows where they are. It was a top-secret document, and I seriously doubt he gave them to anybody. Maybe the recipes will go to whoever buys the business."

But as Esteban contorted his face into a shit-eating grin, he declared, "I happen to know where Harvey's recipes are."

Maria was shocked to hear Esteban's claim. "But ... what do you mean? How ...?"

"How is it possible? How do I *know* where his recipes are?" Esteban thoughtfully tilted his head and explained, "I can only define it as destiny. It was as if it was meant to be and fate looked favorably upon us that day, and I think even Harvey's subconscious drove him to reveal the whereabouts of this prized possession to us."

"Oh my God, Esteban. What did you do?"

"I didn't do anything, Maria. When I visited him in the hospital, they were only allowing one person into the room at a time, and I went by his bedside and …" Esteban paused for dramatic effect.

"And then? And then what?" yelled Miguel as he took Esteban by the shoulders and shook him. "Then what?"

"Well, he was obviously in a state of confusion, and I think he thought I was his brother, and he asked me to lean closer to his mouth, and he told me where I, aka Harvey's brother, could find his recipe book if anything happened to him and he didn't make it."

With stunned expressions on their faces, they cried out in unison, "Where are the recipes?"

"The only thing I will tell you is that they're at his house. I won't tell you more than that. I don't want you morally compromised with what I'm going to do."

"His house? In a safe? How are we going to get into his house? You can't break in, Esteban," declared Maria.

"Of course I'm not going to break in, Maria. Are you crazy? Anyway, I don't have to, because we're going to his house tomorrow."

"To sit Shiva?" contributed a pensive Miguel. "We're going to sit Shiva. Already?"

"Yeah. It starts tomorrow afternoon, after they're done with the burial. I figured we could go after the shop closes."

· · ·

As they arrived at the Shiva the next afternoon, Esteban provided instructions to Maria and Miguel for the precarious undercover operation. Although the three were nervous and exhibited mixed feelings regarding their attempt at corporate spying, they proceeded with unabated commitment and confidence. "OK, I'm going to make believe that I have to go to the bathroom. You guys mingle and be my decoy, and don't forget to act like you're grieving. I need like ten minutes and I'll meet you back here."

Maria and Miguel discreetly collected something to eat and then started their conversational assault on the assembled mourners while Esteban went on his mission. Within ten minutes he was back, and the three Cubans offered their sympathies to Harvey's widow, saying how much they and his friends would miss him, and discreetly left.

"OK, what happened in there, Esteban?"

"Well, I went into his den, went to the bookshelves behind his desk, and there it was, right where he said it would be, right between Mark Twain's *Huckleberry Finn* and Agatha Christie's *And Then There Were None*. I couldn't believe it. Opportunity staring me square in the face."

Miguel questioned their moral authority. "I can't believe we did this. I can't believe it. We go to a dead man's house. A guy—a colleague, in fact—who died just a couple of days ago, and while we attend his Shiva in his home, we steal a prized recipe book that he regarded to be as special as the Ark of the Covenant."

"I feel a little weird about it now. It's a little weird, ain't it? I mean, you talk about blood money in this business, but you've taken it to a whole other level, Esteban," said Maria.

"Listen, you two, Harvey was a great guy and

everything, and he made a helluva good rugelach, and I am sure he would have liked us to have his recipes. Also, this is business, so I was just acting on his last wishes—"

Miguel interrupted, "Yeah, Esteban, but you said he must have thought you were his brother when he told you."

"Miguel, maybe he did, maybe he didn't. Whatever it was, he told me where the recipe book was for a reason, whether he thought I was his brother or not. No one will ever know. And remember the first *Godfather* movie when Michael Corleone told his brother Sonny, 'It's nothing personal, Sonny, it's just business'? That's what this was. We acted on a business tip."

"So you have the book?" interjected Miguel.

Esteban looked insulted. "What is wrong with you, dude? I didn't steal the book."

"Oh, thank God. I would hate for us to make money off of someone's dead back."

"I would never steal the book, and truthfully it was more like a little journal. No, no, no. That's so unethical I don't even want to think about it."

Miguel was not immune to Esteban's sense of indignity at the thought of any ethical breach of decorum on his part.

Esteban recovered his composure and continued, "I took the book from the shelf, went to the bathroom, locked the door, and photographed it— every recipe and even some new ones he hadn't started making yet for a new line of babkas. I then returned it to where I had found it."

An astonished but equally impressed Miguel responded, "You photographed the recipes? Like in a spy movie?"

Esteban nodded affirmatively.

"Oh, that's different, then. That's fine. As long as you didn't actually steal the book."

"Like I said, Miguel, the book is back where Harvey said it was, and I have the pictures to prove it!"

In unison, Miguel and Maria shouted, "Look out, world! We're in the rugelach business, baby!"

Vignettes

In which the main characters insisted a few anecdotes be included.

Cuban Bread and the James Beard House

A luscious red tomato sauce sat simmering in a pot on a stove. The seductive garlic-and-red-pepper fragrance rose slowly with the steam, indicative of a creole sauce.

"Whaddya think of that?" bellowed a proud Chef Daniel as he enthusiastically pointed at the pot adjacent to a freshly baked loaf of Cuban bread.

"Lookin' good, Big D. Lookin' nice," responded Miguel. He leaned over the pot, drinking in the aroma and salivating with expectation. "What are you makin'?"

"Camarónes enchiladas, tostones, maduros, arroz blanco, and frijoles negros."

"Damn. You can't get more Cuban than that."

The culinary theme for the evening was Cuban food, and Chef Daniel was the featured chef, on stage to prepare a private dinner service for a gang of haughty Manhattan foodies at the legendary James

Beard House. Big D, as he was affectionately known, was a Cuban guy the size of an offensive lineman who clearly enjoyed indulging in whatever he prepared for someone else, and his personality was as robust as his size. It became quickly apparent that the basement kitchen in the James Beard brownstone, although exquisitely designed, was not meant to accommodate guys the size of Big D.

Maria had secured the elusive invite for Big D at the iconic gastronomic venue and was upstairs schmoozing with members of its foundation. Unfortunately, she had made what she felt to be a reasonable adult decision to leave Miguel and Big D downstairs by themselves.

Big D poured two shots of tequila and they toasted to the occasion, and quickly followed with two more shots from the bottle.

"Oh shit—that's good stuff, Miguel," Big D said as he smiled profusely and proceeded to rip the head off the Cuban loaf. He handed the head to Miguel, then ripped off another chunk of loaf and savagely immersed his piece in the sauce.

"Whaddya waitin' for?" prompted Big D, chomping on his now-retrieved sauce-soaked bread. "Put in the whole piece so you don't double-dip, Miguel."

As Miguel submerged his piece in the sauce, they were surprised by a cackling of voices that soon grew louder. "Right this way. Right this way." Miguel recognized the voice of the foundation's director, who was evidently leading an entourage of diners. Miguel was forced to surrender his bread to the sauce in order to wave hello.

"This is Chef Daniel, everyone. Chef Daniel, we are so excited to have you here and are excited about what we'll be enjoying for dinner tonight. Would you mind sharing what to expect for our dinner, please?"

"Of course. Good evening, everyone." Big D went on to tantalize his audience, explaining the evening's fare in exotic detail. Perceiving that his audience was mesmerized by his romantic Cuban culinary musings, he decided to employ his long-standing test to see if these diners were authentic foodies or only pretend food lovers. He would give one guest a chance to sample his cuisine.

"Would you like to try the sauce?" he said, offering a chunk of the Cuban loaf to one of the guests. "Just take the piece and dunk it right in."

The guest flinched uncomfortably at the offer, muttering, "Now? You mean dip it … right in the sauce, Chef Daniel?" He floated his face above the sauce until his nostrils visibly twitched, then declined after looking at his host as if for permission. "I'd rather not ruin my dinner, chef, but thank you so very much anyway, my dear."

The group was escorted out of the kitchen. Miguel and Big D burst out laughing and poured another shot of tequila.

Maria appeared in the kitchen doorway. "What are you guys up to?" she asked rather skeptically.

"Where'd you come from?" asked Miguel.

"Let's go upstairs. They're seating everybody. Daniel, you all set?"

"Hundred percent, Maria. I'll send you up a shot, Miguel."

"Isn't this gorgeous?" whispered Maria as they stepped into the opulent dining room.

"A bit stuffy, maybe?" squirmed Miguel. "It's like a monastery."

"It is a culinary monastery, you barbarian," kidded Maria.

The first serving came to their table, accompanied by an additional plate that was placed by Miguel. It was the drenched piece of Cuban bread that he had left in the saucepot when they were interrupted by the foodie tour. Teddy, the waiter, leaned in close to Miguel and said, "Chef Daniel said you were soaking this in the enchilada sauce and left it behind. He said it was now perfect and wanted you to have it."

What Time Does the Concert Start?

It was eleven at night, and Esteban had been driving around a seedy neighborhood in the Lower East Side of Manhattan, near Greenwich Village, for more than half an hour. He was looking for a venue that was hosting a Latin rock concert.

"This doesn't look good," a concerned Esteban expressed to his wife. "Are we in the right area, Marylin?"

They were patrolling the neighborhood because Marylin owned a prominent marketing firm that specialized in Hispanic advertising and had secured a contract to promote a Latin rock band on their inaugural tour of some US cities. Their kickoff concert was taking place in the bowels of "underground NY," in a once-reputable theater that had been transformed into a chic but obscure entertainment lounge. In fact, it was so "underground" it did not have any signage or a marquee. The owners subscribed to the theory that if you didn't know where it was, then you didn't belong there.

"There's no one on the streets. I don't even see homeless people around. Even they're too scared to be around here," continued a now-exasperated Esteban. "And no parking garages anywhere. But then, why would there be parking garages around here at all?"

"I know it's around here. They said it's on 4th Street near Avenue B," responded Marylin, as she intently scanned the garbage-ridden streets.

"And we ARE NOT leaving the car somewhere, or walking around here. The car'll get broken into or we'll be mugged."

"Esteban, shut up, please, and help find this place. I have to be there, OK? So shut up and look."

Two weeks earlier, Marylin had arrived home jubilantly proclaiming that she had secured a liquor company to sponsor her Latin rock concert tour concept. "The whole thing, Esteban!" she said as she performed jumping jacks while clenching the contract in her right hand as if it were the Olympic torch. "A five-city tour! The whole thing!"

"Wow, congratulations! That's a hell of a thing to pull off. Great job."

"The first concert is right here, in a theater by the Village, in two weeks."

"I'll go with you. We'll make a night of it to celebrate. Nice dinner in Little Italy and then we'll go to the concert."

Esteban was unaware of the nightlife that awaited him, and he mentally calibrated that he would organize the evening's festivities as they had always done when going into the city to see plays or musicals, where they were both happily in bed by eleven p.m. Eleven thirty at the latest. The day before the concert, he told Marylin he'd made dinner reservations at Pomodoro Rosso.

"Pomodoro's? Wow! How'd you pull that off? It's the hottest ticket in town."

"I have my magical ways, Marylin. That's how I *tricked you* into marrying me."

"What time are the reservations?"

"Six thirty, and then after dinner, we slide right into the concert."

"Six thirty? What do you mean, six thirty?"

Esteban was perplexed. "Six thirty, Marylin. Same time as we do every time we catch a play or a musical."

"Esteban, this is a concert someplace in the Village. What time do you think it starts?"

"Eight thirty?" Esteban shrugged.

"Eight thirty? Have you ever been to *The Rocky Horror Picture Show* in the Village?"

"Well, no."

"It starts at midnight. Do you know what time this concert starts?"

"No, but we're usually home by eleven."

"The band goes onstage around midnight."

"Oh." Esteban was careful not to appear traumatized at the news.

"So, what are we going to do between six thirty and midnight?"

"I'll change the reservations to nine thirty."

Following their celebrated late-night dinner, Esteban and Marylin got into their car and began their scavenger hunt for the club, navigating through the threatening section of town referred to as Alphabet City.

"There, there!" exclaimed Marylin, excitedly pointing to a stylishly dressed tall, burly Black man illuminated by a streetlight. He had emerged out of what appeared to be a dilapidated building decorated with various types of refuse.

"How the fuck could that be the place, Marylin? It looks like a shithole."

"Well, let's see. It's eleven thirty and he's the only living being on the streets."

"Yeah, and he is one huge dude."

"And he's got a headset on, Esteban. I think this is the place."

They watched as he began setting up stanchions, the kind typically used to organize patrons entering a venue.

"Oh shit. I think you're right. But there's still no place to park. I'm not parking on any street around here. Our car will be stripped in thirty seconds."

"How about you give this guy—the bouncer or whatever he is—some money and ask him to watch our car while we go see the concert. We'll park it right outside. We're only going to be there for an hour, maybe."

Esteban looked at Marylin approvingly, and they approached the burly guy, who confirmed it was the venue they were looking for and that the concert would start at twelve thirty. The man also agreed to watch the car—for fifty dollars. Esteban thought it was worth every penny.

Esteban and Marylin lost their breath when they entered the theater. It had been palatially transformed with elegant white lounge sofas and high-top tables, all accented with thin white sails and soft candle-like white lights. It was an oasis in a desert of the destitute. The band climbed onstage at one a.m., and Esteban and Marylin danced to the infectious Latin rhythms until four in the morning. Then they went for breakfast.

I'm Going to Kneel and Pray That You Punch Me in the Face

Startled, Miguel bristled at the shrieks coming from the front door and jumped out of his chair, alarmed, to see what was going on. He was disturbed to see his seven-year-old son, Jaime, bawling uncontrollably as he ran into Miguel's arms.

"Hijo, what happened?" he asked, grabbing Jaime by the shoulders.

"Guillermo ... Guillermo!" screamed his son between sobs.

Guillermo, thought Miguel. Then he said, "What about Guillermo?"

Jaime's schoolmate, Guillermo, was a mischievous youngster known to have bully tendencies. Although Guillermo was the shortest boy in his entire grade, he had gained a well-earned reputation for reckless behavior where he would inexplicably attack other students on a whim.

"We were playing, and he got mad and then he hit me a bunch of times!"

"Did you do anything to—"

"No, Papi. I didn't do anything to make him mad at me."

"OK, OK. Stop crying, Jaime. It's alright," consoled Miguel. "We're going to fix this right now."

As Jaime wiped away his tears, Miguel got down on both his knees to face his son.

"Papi, what are you doing?"

"I want you to punch me in the face."

Jaime thought his father was making a joke to help him feel better, but that was not the case.

"What?"

"I know it sounds strange, but punch me in the face."

The young boy hesitated, thinking his father was kidding.

"C'mon. Punch me in the face. Don't worry. I am not going to get angry with you, but I will get angry if you don't punch me."

Jaime reluctantly proceeded to delicately slap

Miguel on his left cheek and waited for the response.

"No. Not like that. I want you to make a fist. I want you to wind up like you're throwing a football and punch me right here," Miguel said, pointing to his jaw. "Don't be afraid."

Jaime generated a little more enthusiasm on his second try, but it still wasn't forceful enough for Miguel.

"OK. That was a little better, but try again and this time you need to punch me as hard as you can. I'm not going to move. Don't hesitate, and let me have it like you're Batman punching the Joker."

On his third attempt, Jaime curled his hand into a fist, leaned back, and unleashed a fist of fury that landed squarely on Miguel's jaw. Miguel registered a look of surprise and then shook his head. The shocked son looked at his father, fearing he had hurt him and would be punished. Instead, Miguel straightened up, rubbed his jaw, and congratulated his son.

"Excellent. Good job. Do you know why I wanted you to punch me in the face?"

The perplexed boy shook his head.

"Because I wanted you to actually feel what it's like to punch someone in the face. The next time Guillermo throws one of his tantrums and tries to hit you, you just punch him square in his face. OK?"

"But that will hurt him …"

"Correct. It will hurt him and he won't try to hurt you again. And this goes for anyone that tries to hurt you. Defend yourself and punch them in the face as hard as you can, and they will never bother you again."

The next morning, Miguel left on a two-day business trip. When he returned, Maria met him as he came through the front door.

"I didn't want to call you while you were away, but

I had to go to the principal's office."

"Why?"

"Because our son punched Guillermo in the face and gave him a bloody nose."

"Oh, is that all?" Miguel's pride in his son showed on his face. "What did you say to the principal?"

"I told her it was just a matter of time, because Guillermo has been acting aggressively with my son, and others as well."

"What did she say?"

"Incredibly, she actually understood and said that she would speak to Guillermo's parents about his behavior."

"Good. About time."

"But, Miguel ... our son told me that you told him to punch Guillermo in the face. Did you know about this? Did you have anything to do with it?"

"Maria, I showed our son how to defend himself. I'm not going to let him be bullied. He has to stand up to bullies for his own good."

"And you taught him to defend himself?"

"You betcha!" he proudly exclaimed, not knowing quite what to expect from his spouse.

Maria kissed him, gave him a playful left to the jaw, smiled, and sashayed away.

Later in the afternoon, Miguel heard Jaime coming in from school. "Oh shit," he muttered, fearing the unexpected. However, Jaime ran happily into Miguel's arms. "Papi! You're home!"

"Hijo, is everything OK? How's school?"

"Everything is great, Papi."

"And Guillermo?"

"He started a fight with me *again*, and I just punched him in the face like you said."

"And … what happened?"
"I hit him in the nose and he started to bleed."
"Is he OK?"
"Yup. He's coming over to play."
"He's coming here? To play?"
"Yup. We're best friends."

Acknowledgments

My wife continues to support me like she did when we got married in 1991, and she inspires me every day I wake up next to her. Thank you, honey.

I'm blessed to have the renewed support of Life to Paper Publishing and its stellar team, including Tabitha Rose and Don Loney. Special shout-out to Don: thank you for sharing your experience and comic range. I enjoyed working with you.

Angel Bernal, thanks for letting me lean on you to filter the first drafts. I appreciate your creative and mental acuity.

About the Author

Elected official. Entrepreneur. Professor. Executive. Professional golfer. A first-generation Cuban-American known for his dynamic storytelling, Eurice E. Rojas has worn many hats. A councilman of Cliffside Park, New Jersey, where he lives with his wife, Norma, Rojas brings a unique blend of expertise, creativity, and strategic thinking to everything he does. In his first book, *Out of the Rough: The Cuban Revolution and Its Effect on Golf,* he detailed the story of his father's relationship with Castro and being a political prisoner, his escape from Cuba, and how they built a new life in New York City. Rojas is an alumnus of DePaul University and Seton Hall University. His family's ownership of a traditional bagel shop was his inspiration for *Bagels & Cafecitos*.